SALES, SEX & SALVATION

A salesman's story and search for redemption

KEN OWENSBY

Publishing Coordinator – Sharon Kizziah-Holmes
Cover Design – Jaycee DeLorenzo
Formatting – Ann Yen Gilmore

Paperback-Press
an imprint of A & S Publishing
A & S Holmes, Inc.

ISBN -13: 978-1-951772-76-5

DEDICATION

This book is dedicated to my grandmother, God rest her soul after dying at 101 years old. Born in Tallin, Estonia, her husband was ripped away by a foreign power and she was left to escape the country with her daughter and her teen-age sister. My grandmother had a great story to tell, but her generation put the past away and would never speak of it.

To my mom, who inherited her mother's courage and helped me better understand my family's history.

To Hank Chinaski, for inspiration.

Finally, and most importantly, to my loving wife Barb, who never gave up on me despite my countless failures in life. Thank you.

CONTENTS

ACKNOWLEDGMENTS

This book was pushed forward by the help of many people. And "pushed" is exactly what I mean to say. This is my debut novel. First and foremost I had the support of my wife, Barb, who encouraged me to continue at times when I considered giving up. Trish Walker, author of "Oh Honey, I'm Just Getting Started" suggested I get test readers before making the decision to publish the manuscript. Mark McLaughlin, a well-known brand consultant and principle of McLaughlin Strategy, Peter Fitzgerald, a retired Long Island school teacher, and Glenn Dinetz, a former business colleague and adjunct professor at Rutgers School of Criminal Justice, all provided feedback as test readers saying I had an interesting story to tell. Mark McLaughlin worked with me providing invaluable suggestions on ways to improve the readability and develop characters. Peter Fitzgerald provided editing services. Additionally, thank you to Sharon Kizziah-Holmes, my publishing coordinator at Paperback Press, for helping to bring the book to life.

I spent many years in the business world meeting a vast array of unique people. These people fueled the idea of writing this book. While the book is fiction, I borrowed ideas heavily from my years in the business world to come up with ideas to fictionalize. I sincerely hope none of my past colleagues think any of the characters are them. I just tried to have fun with the main character-- with all of his failings-- and the people that he interacted with along his journey.

"Some of it's magic,
And some of it's tragic,
But I had a good life all the way."
Jimmy Buffet from He Went To Paris

SALES, SEX & SALVATION

To start off, you need to know I was a shitty husband for a long time. I didn't intend to be, but as it turned out I had a problem saying "no" to young women who made themselves available to me. My name is Kevin Owens, a perpetual fuck-up trying to find my way back to humanity.

Growing up in a suburb of Akron, OH in the 1970s, I thought life was pretty good. It wasn't until later in life that I came to realize we were on the very bottom of middle class. As I progressed through middle school, I came to know kids from the nice new developments in our little town. Their houses were new. Their parents had two nice cars in their attached two-car garages. They went on vacations to Myrtle Beach, SC and Disneyworld. My parents both worked and lived paycheck to paycheck. From the time I was born until I moved out at nineteen years old, my parents only purchased one brand new car—a modest Chevy sedan. Until I was an adult, my parents didn't have a two-car garage. They had a shabby old one-car garage. We did take vacations when I was a kid, but we only drove to fishing camp in Canada where our entire family of five stayed in the same cabin. My parents did things for us that I still wonder where they found the money, such as buying me a new off-the-road motorcycle when I was still a kid, which started my lifelong passion for motorcycling.

I have a brother, Jimmy, who was thirteen months older, and a sister, Elaine, two years younger. My brother was a star athlete up until his junior year in high school when his partying became much more important than playing sports or even going to classes. He never graduated from high school, as he did not complete the required senior English class. He did twelve years of work just to fail due to one class. He did screw just about every girl he wanted to in high school, though. He and I shared a bedroom in our house. I recall coming home one afternoon as he and his girlfriend of the week came downstairs. I went up to our bedroom to find an empty beer bottle covered in Vaseline® and pubic hair next to his unmade bed. I later asked him about it, and he laughed about them using it as a sex toy. I really didn't want to know who was on the receiving end. I really thought she was a decent girl; one too good for him. I guess she fell for the "star" quality he still had at that point as the starting running back and linebacker. Later he got the girls thanks to his good looks and constant supply of good drugs.

I dated one girl, Lynn, throughout high school. I lost count how many times my brother tried to get her into bed. I felt bad for my parents as their oldest kid was such a screw-up. Their youngest, my sister, idolized her oldest brother, but luckily, she did not follow his path of poor performance in school. She earned a musical scholarship to the same university I attended. I was just the middle child. I was an "A-B" student, decent track and field athlete who lettered three of four years as a pole vaulter and a wrestler. I and never got in any trouble with the exception of one blip, getting Lynn pregnant.

Thanks to a broken condom, we ended up with a high school pregnancy. Neither of us saw any path to keeping the baby, and she opted the terminate the pregnancy. I supported her decision. Terminating a pregnancy is never an easy decision—nor should it be. We talked many hours about it. We looked at a lot of options including adoption, but her family's religious beliefs were very harsh on pre-marital sex. She was very afraid her mother would throw her out of the house if she found out we were having sex, let alone that she got pregnant. Lynn's parents were divorced and her father had not been a part of her life for a very long time. She saw an abortion as the best choice at the time. We got a little smarter and she got on birth control pills, and there were no more worries about unwanted pregnancy.

I came to understand as parents that they struggled with how their kids turned out. One appeared normal, me, and the other two not so much as they were always in trouble.

MY WIFE, MY LIFE

The relationship started out pretty romantic. OK, working at a gas station at nights while going to college full-time in 1979 and being held up by a group of four guys wanted in three states wasn't romantic. Looking down a barrel of a gun will make you think twice about if this is the right job for you, particularly at minimum wage. It led me to quit and take a job working at a hospital in Cuyahoga Falls, Ohio as an orderly on second shift while I went to college during the daytime. I started college as a biology major. Then, I made a brief switch to construction technology, and when I started working at the hospital, I decided I wanted to be an emergency medical technician. To be an EMT, you need to be a fireman first and then an EMT. As such, I was taking classes to get a fire science associate degree.

On a certain unforgettable evening I was assigned to work on a medical floor, Five East, instead of my usual stint in the emergency room or on the orthopedics floor. The orderly on first shift coming off duty told me to check out a girl in 521 Bed 1. I was a little smarter than he was and I read her chart—married, two kids, and about to be transferred to a psychiatric treatment facility. However, the pretty young woman in 521 Bed 2, Beth Watson…well, that was a different story.

She had been admitted the day after her twenty-first

birthday on August 11 for some tests for an intestinal problem. I spent most of my shift talking to her. We just connected on so many levels. It really seemed as if we had known each other for years. I sent her a dozen roses the next day with a "get well" card. She was impressed until unfortunately one of the nurses let her know I was dating someone. I did manage to beg the nursing supervisor to let me work back on Five East that evening and was smooth enough to explain to Beth that the girlfriend was a high school romance that was over. I spent my entire shift in her room talking to her. She captivated me. It was like nothing I'd ever experienced before—the feelings for her were immediately overwhelming.

We talked about where she went to school; it was the next town over from where I grew up. We talked about her family; she was the youngest of four kids. Her dad was an engineer at a large tire manufacturer where he had worked his entire life. We talked about my current situation. I was a college student working full-time and going to school full-time. I drove a red 1963 Volkswagen Bug that had a black wood 4x4 for a front bumper. I told her about how the guys at the street department where I worked in the summers in high school donated an old stop sign that I riveted into place for a passenger floorboard. We covered about every subject you could think of in an eight-hour period. I told her, too, that I had a brother who was a high school drop-out, drug user, alcoholic, had gotten a girl pregnant while in school, and was now married with a daughter. I told Beth about my younger sister and how she idolized my older brother, which was something I never understood. My older brother was abusive toward my sister. Later in life, she told me he sexually abused her. I could not understand why she held him in such high esteem. She was smart, a gifted singer who struggled with her weight. Maybe somehow my brother played on her self-esteem issues. But I digress; I probably should have been reprimanded for not doing my duties that night as I talked to Beth, but I think the head nurse had an idea of where I was and knew I was available if she needed me.

As I was about to get off at 11:30 pm, I asked Beth, "If you were to get married, do you think you'd want to marry someone like me?"

Beth simply said, "Things like this don't happen this fast."

I was crushed. I crawled out to my car and headed for my parents' home.

The next day, my day off, I mustered up the courage to go back to the hospital and to ask for an answer to my proposal. Had I really proposed? Did Beth take it as a marriage proposal?

On the way, I stopped at the house of my girlfriend of almost four years. I knocked on the front door. Lynn answered, and I simply said, "I cannot see you anymore" and left. How can you tell the first girl you ever had sex with, the girl you once got pregnant thanks to a broken condom, the girl who saw you as the escape from her own dysfunctional family, that you met the woman you wanted to spend your life with less than twenty-four hours ago? I had told Lynn I loved her probably a thousand times in the almost four years we had dated. Hell, when a high school guy is getting sex from a girl routinely, he'll say pretty much anything to keep it coming. And we did have a lot of sex. She'd been my first.

I had never seen the young woman of twenty-one who I think I proposed to stand up or dressed in non-hospital clothes. I knew Beth was two years older than I was, where she worked, and a lot about her family, but that was about all. When she did stand up, I learned she was taller than me by about an inch. It was a surprise as Lynn, my now ex-girlfriend, was much shorter than myself.

I asked about my proposal, and Beth made me get down on one knee later that same day in the hospital room and do a proper one, to which she said "yes." I was ecstatic. Something told me the stars had aligned at just the right time, that our paths were destined to cross and forever become entwined. She was released from the hospital the next day, and I was there to follow her home to her parents' house.

Beth had an apartment in a nice high-rise building in Akron, OH she shared with a friend, but her parents wanted her to stay with them for a bit while she recovered. I got lost following her home, and I was convinced I would never see her again. Luckily, I was fairly good with directions and I found their house.

Things were interesting at first with both sets of our parents. I had met with Louise and James, Beth's parents, the day Beth got out of the hospital. She was still staying at their house and I became a constant fixture there when I was not at college or work. At dinner one evening with her parents about two weeks after she'd been released from the hospital, Beth simply said "Mom, Dad, we are going to get married. We're engaged!" and at that she brought forth the small diamond engagement ring I'd been able to purchase with my last nickel.

She had been with me at the jewelry store and selected her setting. I insisted I would pay for it all. I had grown up in a family that didn't have much money, and it was very important for me to pay for my bride's engagement ring. My mom never had an engagement ring, only a simple wedding band. I wanted more for my bride-to-be. I had a credit card, which I put some of the cost of the ring on, and paid for the rest with a few hundred dollars I'd withdrawn from my meager savings account.

James, Beth's dad, was a warm and friendly man who was about to retire. He was calm and never got too up or down about anything. He looked at me and said, "You're going to take care of my little girl, aren't you?"

I told him, "I know it looks like I don't have much, sir, but I am working hard to make something of myself. I think as a team, we can conquer the world together."

He turned and looked at his wife and, without waiting for her input, simply said, "Well, then, you have our blessing. When is the wedding?"

We started talking about what we had in mind and plans began to form. I had been so warmly welcomed into Beth's family. I was very surprised how well they took the news considering the fact Beth and I had only met about two weeks before. She was the youngest of four kids. Maybe they were just glad to see the last kid be on her own, not that she had been living with them anyhow.

While Beth's parents readily accepted me into the family, it wasn't so on my side. The night I met Beth, I came home and sat down with my parents.

"Mom, Dad, I met an incredible woman tonight at work. I am in love!"

"At work?" my dad replied. "Is she a nurse?"

"No, she is a patient. Her name is Beth. She has the most beautiful blue eyes I have ever seen. She's elegant, funny, engaging, and so many things I can't even describe," I gushed on.

"Don't be stupid," my mom shot back. "You are already dating a great girl. Don't be stupid and think you are going to marry her."

I did my best to ignore her comment and not tell them I thought I had already proposed. They would find out soon enough.

I moved in with Beth as soon as she returned to her apartment. We agreed not to have intercourse until the wedding, which was only about six months away. Beth had never been sexually active and was very worried about getting pregnant. Given my one very fateful experience in high school with Lynn, I was determined not to have an unplanned pregnancy either. We became very intimate in other ways. It was a wonderful and romantic opportunity to learn about things she liked sexually without actually having sex itself. Beth was able to explore things that were new to her without pressure and fear of pregnancy.

It all was going as planned until Yom Kippur, which was in early October and a few months before we were to be married in March. I had a professor cancel my last class when a student protested that the Christian students got their holidays off but not the Jewish students. The professor agreed and cancelled class. I found a payphone and called Beth to let her know I was coming home early. I also had the evening off work.

She said, "Pick up some condoms on your way home. I'm ready."

I was floored, but I didn't have a nickel on me and these was the days before ATMs, plus I didn't carry my credit card with me. I ran into a friend from high school attending the same university and asked if I could borrow five dollars.

He said, "What for?"

"Gas for the car" was my quick reply. I really couldn't tell him I was buying condoms to go home to have sex. He loaned me a five and I stopped at a drug store before heading for Beth's apartment.

I don't remember the first time I had sex with Lynn. We had made several fumbled attempts in the backseat of my 1964 Mercury before we figured it out. But at least with Beth, there would be a specific moment when we decided to be really intimate with each other. It would be a special day that we would both remember. There would be a day on the calendar every year in October that marked the anniversary. Sure, Yom Kippur doesn't fall on the exact same day every year, but it would be symbolic for us for all our life together.

When I arrived, I said, "Why did you change your mind and decide to not wait until the wedding?"

Beth simply said, "I know I love you and a few more months isn't going to change that. I know who I want and I want to be with you now."

I recall she was wearing a perfume I'd gotten her as a gift. The sweet smell of that perfume lingered gently in the air as I took in her words. We moved into the bedroom of her apartment. We slowly undressed, softly touching each other. The late afternoon sun came in through the sheer curtains on the seventh-floor windows, casting long shadows across the bed. I wanted her first time to have more memories than just the intercourse. I wanted her to know love and tenderness. She was a virgin and didn't know what to expect. I didn't want this to seem like a cheap conquest, like something my brother Jimmy would do when he robbed the virginity from so many girls he had no feelings for.

I tried to go slow and gentle, but within moments I quickly had an orgasm. It had been several months since I had made love, and I had been ready to explode.

Beth said, "Is that all there is? I expected more."

I felt so much like I had disappointed her. I shed the filled condom, got a new one, and started over for a much longer session. She seemed much more satisfied with the extended lovemaking.

Maybe I was being a bit too self-critical. Anytime a woman says, "I expected more," a man immediately questions a lot of things. Was his size not enough? Was he too fast in finishing? Was he too rough? Was he not rough enough? In reality most young men are very insecure about sex, myself included. I just wanted to please Beth.

I'd like to say she moaned with delight, but first-time sex for most women, from what I'm told, isn't all that magical. What was important to me was that the young woman I'd so quickly fallen in love with wanted to share her body with me in the most intimate way possible. But I still feel bad her first time ended with the thought of, "Is that all there is?"

We started to talk after making love. Beth wasn't one to talk about sex. It was difficult to get her to talk much, but the floodgates finally opened.

"I have been hit on by so many guys, had so many men try to get my clothes off after a date. I felt like a piece of meat so many times. You were willing to wait until I said I was ready. You never pressured me into anything. I think that is how you showed me you loved me the most."

I wasn't sure how to respond. After a moment, I said, "Beth, I fell in love with you from the first moment I saw you. If you would have told me I had to wait a year to make love to you I would have waited."

"How did you know?" she asked, her fingers curling around mine.

"I can't explain it. It was just a feeling that came over me. I know that I needed to be with you, and I felt like you needed me as well."

"You're crazy. You know that, don't you?" she laughed.

The mood went from serious to playful in a heartbeat. "Yeah, who's nuts? Maybe the pretty young woman who left some guy who she barely knows into her apartment to have sex with her and then marry him?"

"OK, we'll call this one even," she smiled and gave me a kiss.

We started talking about our future together. It was the first time I'd ever had a discussion like this. Lynn and I had talked about getting married while in high school but it had been so far off and not real. It had just been two high school kids talking. This was real. This was happening. We talked about where we would be living. We talked about jobs and what my career would be. We pulled out my backpack and looked at the college credits I had accumulated starting off as a biology major, then switching to construction technology and finally to fire science technology.

My idea of becoming an EMT first didn't sit well with Beth. She wasn't fond of the idea of her husband being at a fire station two days on and one day off constantly. Beth and I pulled out the college class guide and determined if I took a heavy load of computer programming classes over the summer, I could earn an associate's degree in computer science. I could then take additional classes at night once I was working to complete my bachelor's degree in business.

I didn't know a thing about computer programming, but I wanted my bride-to-be to feel safe and secure in what I was doing, and I'd heard there was pretty good money in computer programming. The decision was made to switch my major. It's funny how monumental decisions happen without warning. When I woke up that morning, I had no idea Beth would decide to make love to me for the first time and that I would end up on a career path that would take me into so any perils.

It really was a miracle Beth and I ever connected. She a little older than I and a little taller. I wore faded blue jeans and either a flannel shirt or some worn, printed T-shirt to college during the day. In the evening I changed into my hospital uniform of a blue short-sleeve cotton button-up shirt, white slacks and white tennis shoes. They were good leather adidas® Stan Smiths, as I was a bit of a tennis player. They would eventually become stained with too much blood from the many tragic things I witnessed as an orderly working on second shift in the emergency room. Rules of who can do what get tossed aside when a patient comes in with a gunshot wound to the head or that ran into a cement truck head-on in an MG Midget.

The hospital was a great place for a young guy to learn things. You learned if you chug down an entire bottle of a hundred-proof vodka all at once, you will die of acute alcohol poisoning. You learn if you put a .38 caliber gun to the side of your head and pull the trigger in an attempt to commit suicide, you might not die. Some young orderly might just have to scrape brain matter off your head as you go into surgery. You may live, leaving yourself really messed up and get arrested for attempted murder when you finally get released from the hospital months later. Laws in the 1970s about attempted suicide were different then. Today people trying to commit suicide are put into mental health facilities. Back in the old days, if you didn't succeed, you were charged with attempted murder is some states. You learn that even though parents love their little children more than themselves, sometimes they get sick or into accidents and they die no matter how hard the doctors and nurses try to save them. You also learn that even if you are really drunk and there is a lot of cooking oil on it, sticking a light bulb up your ass on a dare by your buddies is a bad and embarrassing idea. You will get a bit sober at some point and the light bulb is still going to be up your ass, and what do you do now? You go to the emergency room begging them not to break it and shred your rectum into hamburger. I recall how terrified and how humiliated the guy was when he had to bend over an examination table to show the attending physician his predicament. It would be a scene I would never forget. Your actions had consequences. Maybe every nineteen-year-old kid should have to work in an ER for a few months just to get ready for what the real word is going to hand out at some point.

Beth was an administrative assistant at the same company her dad worked for. She worked in the legal department where she was the hot young babe every single and many married lawyers wanted to screw. She told me of being hit on countless times by single and married men alike. Sometimes it was subtle, other times blatant. She had told me of an older attorney actually trying to put his hand under her dress while she was at the copy machine. It was the late 1970s and no one in Human Resources wanted to hear a pretty young clerical make a complaint against the corporate attorneys. She was tall and had beautiful legs. She was slim and had killer blue eyes with stunning blond hair worn in the Farrah Fawcett style that was ever so popular at the time. She was the type of young woman who turned heads. She dressed in tight-fitting knit dresses that were popular in the late 1970s. She had dated a few of the attorneys from the law department. One collected Corvettes. These guys made salaries I could only dream of making some day. They lived in parts of town I'd only been to as a laborer when I worked for a friend's dad's heating and cooling company. Beth went out to discos and clubs that were hot back in the day. The clubs and particularly discos were never my thing. During college I was more of a jeans, flannel shirts, cheap beer, and John Denver kind of guy. I drove a beat-up Bug and she had a nice new blue Camaro.

Had we ever met outside of that hospital room, I am sure she never would have given me a second glance. Well, maybe a second glance as I did have pretty awesome blond hair. It would not have gone any further. But there we were in that hospital room, stripped of our normal clothes and surroundings, just talking to each other, and we connected in a manner of hours. We both knew we belonged together and would get married from the moment we met.

Unfortunately, during my early days with Beth, my ex-girlfriend Lynn wouldn't go away. She and my mom had been very close. Lynn decided all of a sudden that she would become my sister's best friend. Lynn left love notes at my parents' house for me. It finally got to the point where I had to have a "come-to-Jesus" meeting with my family.

I said to my mom, "Mom, your relation with Lynn is damaging your relationship with my fiancée. You need to make a choice about whom you want in your life. Beth and me or Lynn."

My mom pushed back, "You don't even know Beth. You've been with Lynn for so many years. You two have been through so much together. How could you do this to her?"

"Mom, this isn't about Lynn," I said. "It was a high school romance. It ran its course and it's over. I fell in love with Beth and we are getting married. Either you and dad are going to be part of our lives or you can have Sunday dinners with Lynn."

They had to choose one or the other because it wasn't going to be both. They finally broke off their relationship with Lynn.

Beth and I were married five months later during my sophomore year of college. We went on to have a great honeymoon in the Caribbean when most of my college buddies were in places like Myrtle Beach or Fort Lauderdale hoping to get laid by some drunken girl they could somehow talk back to their hotel room. I, on the other hand, was nursing a nasty sunburn but having sex twice a day with the most beautiful woman in the world, enjoying lobster and tropical drinks.

Well, it wasn't completely over with Lynn. Lynn decided to get married. She asked my younger sister, whom she had not really been friends with until we broke up, to be a bridesmaid. She wanted my older brother to drive them from the church to the reception in my 1957 Fury. Lynn and I had used my '57 Plymouth, which I had restored, to drive to the high school homecoming, winter formal, and prom. It was my special occasion car. From the outside it was beautiful, but I still needed to restore the interior. I declined to have my antique car used for my ex-girlfriend's wedding. She was not going to make her wedding memories in my and now my wife's car, especially with my brother driving it. He was now heavy into booze and hard-core drugs. There was no way he was getting behind the wheel of my Plymouth.

My parents were invited to the wedding. I was still working second shift at the hospital the evening of the wedding. Beth got a call around 4:00 pm from Lynn's sister.

"Lynn isn't at the church. She left her fiancé standing at the altar. She didn't show up. Do you know where she is?"

"How the hell would I know where she is? I don't speak to her."

"Is Kevin home? Maybe he knows where she is?"

"No," Beth said, "and quit calling us!"

I got home from work around midnight having driven home in a hard rain and Beth started telling me about the bizarre phone call, our phone rang. I answered. I heard Lynn say, "I only agreed to marry him to get back at you" and she hung up.

I knew I'd married the right woman.

The first year or two of marriage was more like an extended dating period where I knew I was going to have sex most every night. We were living in an inexpensive twin-plex near the high school I had attended, next to Mary and her husband Bob, who was going blind. Bob owned a twenty-eight-foot sailboat that he had at a slip up on Lake Erie. He begged me to go sailing with him frequently.

Bob had macular degeneration, which eliminates your forward vision, leaving you with only peripheral vision. Beth and I would go up to the lake with Bob and Mary, and I would get the boat out of the slip and steer it out of the harbor. Once in open waters, Bob could use his remaining vision to sail. He so loved to sail. The open waters of Lake Erie were exhilarating. Neither Beth nor I had ever been in a sailboat before. The wind driving the boat through the water with only the sound of the waves around us was so calming. The waters of the lake were different even from the largest lakes I'd fished on in Canada. They seemed to go on forever.

Bob tried so hard to get me to buy his boat and teach me to sail just so he could keep sailing with me. I would have loved to own that boat, but I was broke. To top it off, interest rates at that time for the purchase of a boat would have been around twenty-five percent with the best of credit. We could barely afford a steak dinner for two a couple of times a year, let alone payments on a sailboat. Instead, Beth and I went to high school football games, and we walked to the local ice cream shop through the elementary school yard where we would stop and swing on the swings and go down the slides. We'd play tennis on the high school courts near our place. Beth was a terrible player, but I tried to be patient with her, teaching her basic strokes I learned in my college P.E. class I had taken the semester before we met.

My income had been cut as I was only working part-time at the hospital so I could take on a heavier load to get my computer science degree faster. Still, it was a very care-free time. We would take long drives in my VW with John Denver playing on the stereo that I'd installed in the old Bug. It just seemed to be more fun going on drives to nowhere in the Bug. Beth's Camaro was much nicer, but there was something fun about the old beat-up Bug. Beth had not been a big John Denver fan before I met her, but I was getting her interested in his music. Sadly, John Denver had already passed away two years before Beth and I met, so we would never get to go to see him in a concert together.

My first job out of college was with a large steel company that had a small electronic division that was one of the first to make automatic teller machines, or ATMs. It was a highly technical programming job as there was no Internet, and computers did not have the memory capacity anywhere close to what we walk around with what is inside even the cheapest phones today. The company's primary business was making vault doors and safes for banks. They were a heavy-steel manufacturing firm. We were this crazy electronics division. The company held "foremen's clubs" several times a year for employees above a certain pay grade. I made the cut. I quickly learned the goal of these events was drinking and more drinking. As they were held mostly thirty or more miles from where I lived, I figured out quickly that these club events could be life-threatening. But I was young and wanted to fit in.

I devised a plan. I hated gin. I planned to get a gin and tonic with a lime at the beginning of the events, then sip it slowly or maybe even dump a bit out. I would then just get some ice, refreshing the drink throughout the event. The cocktail with the wedge of lime and smell of gin looked like a real "grown-up" drink, and I would not be shit-faced at the end of the events. I'd make it home without a DUI or ending up dead. It worked, except, as I found out later in life, gin is an acquired taste, and I acquired a taste for it.

With me working at my first job and Beth still working, we bought our first starter home. It was a small two-bedroom ranch in the town where I grew up. It needed a lot of work and we put a lot of sweat equity into the place. It did not have a garage, though, something both of us wanted.

After three years of marriage and our second year in our starter home, we decided to start a family in December. Beth immediately became pregnant. As spring came around, I promised her I would build her a two-and-a-half car garage before the baby arrived. I started building in the spring and completed the garage about a week before little Ann arrived in mid-August. We had a fair amount of land, and I had bought a large riding mower with a trailer that I'd put little Ann's car seat in and pull her around the yard as I mowed. It gave Beth a break on Saturdays, as little Ann would sleep through the entire ride. As Ann got a bit older, about two years old, I would take her out for a dad-daughter breakfast every Saturday morning. She would always get hotcakes and never eat too much of them. It was something I really enjoyed, taking my little girl out, just her and I. Being a working mom was tough on Beth, and having a little time to be alone was important.

The downside to working on ATM software is that it was extremely technical and detailed. I was not a detail kind of guy and my work showed it. I, as my business career would prove years later, was a strategic thinker. The firm didn't want strategically thinking ATM programmers. They wanted very detail-oriented programmers. My manager called me into his office one day and told me to close the door.

"Kevin, I am really disappointed in your work. Every project you turn in has errors caught by quality control. At this point I am not sure I can save your job."

I was literally on the verge of being fired. My gut dropped. My mouth went dry. I could not believe what I was hearing. I'd known I'd made some mistakes, but I'd also just been given responsibility to train a newly hired programmer. I thought I was up for a raise and maybe a promotion. Instead, he put me on short-term objectives and I began working sixty hours a week, triple testing every bit of work I did to ensure it met every standard exactly. I pushed out more work faster as well.

Luckily a friend I'd gone to college with contacted me, telling me they had openings at his company for computer programmers. I knew they were an insurance company but I didn't know what I would be doing. I did know it was in the mainstream business world and it had to be better than working on micro computers in a job that I sucked at. I applied at the insurance company. I later learned my manager at the ATM software company had hired many programmers through the same recruiter and gave them all the same speech just as they were coming up for a salary increase. He was later terminated for what everyone suspected of churning through young, inexperienced staff, never having to increase his salary budget. He waited until you were overdue for a salary increase, he would put you on short-term objectives threatening to terminate you, and then he either got a big increase in your production without giving a raise or you quit. Most people quit. It was suspected he was taking kickbacks from the recruiter as well but it was never proven. Welcome to the harsh realities of the business world, Kevin.

I got a job as a computer programmer at the insurance company, but again I quickly discovered I really sucked at testing my work. I was great at meeting with the users, understanding their business needs and then designing systems. I thought I was great at writing the systems. But when it came to testing my work before it went into production, I was a failure. I had the attitude of, "Why does this need so much testing? I wouldn't have written this wrong."

Over-confidence. It is the curse of the youthful. You don't begin to know that you don't know everything until later in life. When you are young, you think you know everything.

About the same time I started my new programming job, we sold our starter home and had a new house built. We found a lot in a nice neighborhood that was one of the two remaining ones the builder had left. He was pulling out and was selling it at a discount. We contracted with another builder and quickly sold our small starter home. In the meantime, we moved in with my mom, who was pretty lonely at this point. My dad had passed away from cancer a few months before and she had never lived in a house by herself in her entire life. My mom had recently retired and was thrilled to have little Ann there with her all day while Beth and I went off to work. It increased my commute to over sixty miles one-way, but the cost savings while we were having the new house built were worth it.

I got a bone tossed my way when an opening became available for an internal auditor. They needed someone with computer systems experience. I wanted out of information technology, or IT, as it was commonly called. Most people looked at internal auditors as terrible people. They are just there to find something wrong and get you fired. In reality, I was lucky to work for Geoff Schinder, whose philosophy was that you didn't always have to have a "finding." When you did audit a department and found a problem, you also had to develop a solution that you would be willing to help implement. By using this philosophy, we were able to gain the trust and respect of department managers and get much greater cooperation in our audits. We also had to thoroughly plan our audits in advance. "Plan the work, work the plan," was Geoff's pet phrase. The time in internal audit was like another business degree for me, but this one was a real, life-learning experience on how a business functions from accounting to operations and everything in between.

MIDDLE AGE

W e went through life like most normal people do. We bought a starter home, we had a child, and we'd moved on to our second larger home. I started to climb the corporate ladder slowly. I started working on an MBA. Beth made some internal moves, leaving the law department and eventually going to a customer service unit that specialized in handling large tire dealers. Unfortunately, Beth's company moved her job to Chicago. She was given the option of moving to Chicago or accepting a severance package. She took the severance package to try out being a stay-at-home mom. The move to internal audit came with a nice increase in pay, which helped offset the loss of Beth's salary. It would be a great training ground for a small company I would eventually own myself. It would also lead me to my first major downfall in my spiral.

I was sent to audit the Palm Sorings, CA office. I would be conducting a full financial, operations, and IT audit myself, solo for the first time. I started in financial and discovered that an insurance agent owed us a significant amount of money. I set up a meeting with the agent, gathered my back-up documentation, and prepared to enlighten him as to why he would be writing us a check for $400,000 that day. But when I confronted him, the guy cut me off and said, "Why the fuck should I give you a dime?"

I started digging into my data reports, but he fired back, "Your system is a piece of shit and your numbers are wrong."

Not what I expected. This son-of-a-bitch was going to make me go through thousands of line-item transactions showing every single dollar we said he owed. It took about a week to do it, but I reconciled every damn dime. And we did get paid. The people in the Palm Springs office thought I was a corporate god.

I became a runner in Palm Springs. I had been on the track team in high school, but I only did pole vault. I had been good at it, but it hadn't required any distance running.

Palm Springs, California had great weather. I woke up around six in the morning, put on some sweats, and headed out for a run. The sun was just beginning to peak up over the desert landscape. The sight of palm trees in the early morning sun was very foreign to me, being from the Midwest. Sand, rocks, and cacti made up the landscape in the undeveloped areas. As the sun rose, the temperatures came up quickly. By the end of my five-mile run, I would be down to my sweatpants. I would be carrying the sweatshirt and T-shirt I had started in. I quickly became lean with a touch of a tan. I wished I had a motorcycle in Pam Desert instead of the boring rental car. I had enjoyed riding so much in my youth and Palm Springs's weather was perfect for motorcycling. It would have given me a relaxing outlet from the stressful days of auditing at the office.

The next step was Operations. I was to go through each department, figure out what they did, why they did it, and if it made sense to do it. I got to one area and met my downfall: Sonja. She was a supervisor to a large number of data entry staff. Sonja and I had lots of discussion about what the department did, but I was just not getting the picture. I felt if I got her out of the office, maybe she would loosen up a bit and I could get the information I needed.

I said, "Sonja, I would like to further the discussion about the department structure, work flow, and goals over dinner. Would you be able to join me? Of course, this would be a business expense. No cost to you."

She was rather shy, but she agreed, and I asked her to bring a notebook so we could record some possible ideas.

The dinner was a bit comical, as Sonja had apparently never eaten in a high-quality restaurant before. She was unaware that the sorbet served between the appetizer and the main course was to cleanse the palate. She thought the lemon sorbet was butter to put on your steak.

We got off to a rocky start, but after a few drinks she started talking shop. I learned more about the real flow of work and what is and what is not done every day. By the end of dinner, I thought Sonja had drank too much to drive safely. We had met at the hotel I was staying at and I offered to book her a room for the night to keep her off the road. She happily agreed.

When we got back to the hotel, it became clear to me she wasn't intoxicated—she was there for a hook-up, with me. She had planned it all along. She even had a convenient overnight bag in her car. She was not going to let me leave the hotel room without having sex with her. I was so naive and so flattered. A young woman coming on to me! This had never happened in my life. I should have just dump her into that room and told her, "Thank you, but I'm married". I will never know why but I let it happen. Maybe I was trying to even up the tally with my brother, who had bedded down so many more girls than I had in high school. I had only been with my high school girlfriend and my wife. My brother had bragged about having had sex with three girls in one day. He routinely rubbed my sexual inexperience in my face whenever he saw me, telling me what a loser I was that no girls wanted to screw me. Now I had the opportunity to prove him wrong.

Sonja pulled her tight-fitting dress over her head and I realized she was not wearing anything under it—no bra, no panties. It was rather an erotic turn-on to such an inexperienced person such as myself. She had a well-toned body. She told me she was a competitive body builder. But it wasn't enjoyable sex, and I did not have an orgasm. I knew it was wrong and I couldn't let myself enjoy it. The excitement of the hunt was fine, but the actual act of intercourse was unsatisfying.

I left quickly, ashamed of what I had let myself do. I thought back to that poor guy who came into the ER with the light bulb in his ass and how humiliated he had been. I had the same feeling of humiliation. I was a fool. I found out later Sonja had a reputation of bedding down men visiting the Palm Springs location from the home office. I heard from another auditor at the home office that it was a bit of a game to her. I guess when you are a young, single person. casual sex can be just for fun.

When I returned home from the trip, I sat down with Beth and admitted to her the terrible mistake I had made.

"Beth, I'd had a few drinks at the hotel bar when this business associate, a young woman, joined me and started talking to me. More drinks came, more talking…somehow, we ended up in my hotel room. I was so far from home and had been away for over almost two months. I'm so sorry. I let things go too far. We ended up back in my room and had sex."

Beth finally responded, "What is her name?"

"Sonja." I replied sheepishly. "This will never happen again, I swear. I will never see her again!"

Beth was cool in her reply. "I love you but I am not going to take this shit. This cannot happen again."

Beth took a long pause before her next words came: "You are not going to make a fool of me in front of my family."

"Beth, we can get through this. It was a one-time

drunken mistake" was my feeble defense I used to assure her.

We talked about it; she was disappointed, and she was angry. I think she believed it was all due to the fact that I had been in Palm Springs for such a long time and she knew I had a very high sex drive. I think it was easier for her to justify my mistake to herself due to the circumstances than to admit that her husband consciously cheated on her. I was surprised Beth didn't threaten to divorce me. As I thought about it more over the days that followed, I began to understand why. People in Beth's family didn't cheat on their spouses. No one got divorced, ever, in the history of her entire family. I am certain she did not want to be the first to have a divorce. I truly believe Beth did not want the embarrassment a divorce would bring on her and her parents. I think she would have preferred to try to work through the mistake than to walk away.

Things were tense at home for a while, but my time at the Palm Springs office was over and I would most likely not be going back any time soon. It helped that the "other woman" was on the other side of the country. Back at the home office at work, I felt like everyone was looking at me differently.

Within a few weeks I applied for an account management position in Albany, New York, getting me out of the home office in Ohio. I was hopeful for a fresh start. But Beth was crushed that we would be leaving the home we had just had built. We had only been in the house eighteen months when I came home to announce that I had secured this account management position in New York. I had not discussed this move with her in advance. I had accepted the offer without so much as even thinking to talk to my wife about packing our little family up and moving to a state we'd only been to on our first anniversary.

All of our family was in Ohio. Our daughter Ann was still in preschool. I did everything I could to convince Beth that moving to New York was a great career move for me. I promised her we'd only be there a short while and then I'd be transferred back to Ohio after I got the large account up and running. In reality I didn't tell her I was running away from my blemished reputation at my employer. Sonja, my mistake in Palm Springs, had a mouth and was happy to tell people at the office that she had had sex with me. Those tidbits worked their way back to the Ohio home office. I was tainted goods in Cleveland. Most people in our division knew Sonja had a reputation for screwing lots of home office guys who went out to the Palm Springs office, even some as high up as the division president. I had to get away.

Beth tried again and again to convince me we didn't need to move. But no, I had it all figured out. Under duress, we moved to Saratoga Springs, New York and bought a house neither of us really liked. The commute to Albany was reasonable and the house was within our price range. And so, I started my career as an account service representative with the firm.

The account was headquartered in Albany about thirty minutes south of our home. It was a pretty good gig. I travelled to each of their banks, managing their start-up of the firm's collateral protection insurance program. The client had banks in New York, Maine, Utah, Idaho, Oregon, Washington, and Alaska. For the shorter trips around New York, I had a company car. When I traveled to Maine, I flew on the client's private plane. Trips to Utah, Oregon, Washington, Idaho, and Alaska were on commercial airlines.

Because I flew often, I frequently upgraded to first class. Unfortunately, I was pretty efficient and got all the banks up and running smoothly in less than eighteen months. My job as account manager was eliminated a few months later. There would be no quick move back to Ohio for us. I was offered a position as a sales representative in the Albany office for another division by my company, but it was a commission-only job. If I turned it down, I received no severance. I negotiated a salary period, saying it would take me some time to build up contacts and get a sales pipeline started. My firm bought the story and agreed to a six-month period of salary that reduced month by month.

Luckily, I was able to land a job as a sales rep with a Miami-based firm immediately that wanted me in their Columbus, Ohio office with a significant base salary and commission. Sadly, I didn't get the relocation terms in writing. Once I realized they were not going to pay for the relocation and simply have me fly from New York to Columbus every week, I started job-hunting again.

This time I landed with a California company that needed someone to cover the New England territory. The money was very good, but we would not be going back to Ohio.

NEW YORK

There were some really great upsides to living in upstate New York. Beth started working at the elementary school where our daughter was attending kindergarten. Beth had never told me she wanted to become a schoolteacher. She graduated third in her high school class but had never gone to college. She had regretted her parents never really opening the door to higher education for her despite her excellent academic performance. Maybe it was because she was their fourth child and they didn't have a college fund for her and her dad was so close to retirement when she graduated from high school. It wouldn't be a topic we ever discussed with them. That door had closed.

The summers in Saratoga Springs were magical. The Saratoga Race Course is a famed thoroughbred horse racing track that originally only ran in the month of August. But while we were living there, the racing schedule expanded to six weeks. Gentlemen wear suit jackets in the grandstand and the ladies generally wear dresses with exquisite hats. The last major thoroughbred race of the season runs there and it is known as the graveyard of champions. Many Triple Crown winners lost their only race at Saratoga. It was fun entertaining clients there. I reported to a young Harvard graduate who was dating the New York racing commissioner's daughter, and he had some pull in getting tickets. If the governor of New York was not at the track, I had access to his box seats. I took Beth and business guests to the governor's box and enjoyed watching people, more so than the horses. I thought maybe those people saw me as a personal friend of the governor. Little did they know I was just a lowly salesman trying to claw his way up the corporate ladder. Having come from such meager beginnings, I was proud of myself; it felt good to feel like I'd achieved some social status my parents had never had in their lives.

"Man and steel rushing through the night to destinations unknown." It was a line I envisioned as the opening line for my first novel. I thought of it in Maine as I was driving back to Saratoga Springs after doing a service call on a bank in Portland, ME. It was somewhat odd that I thought of writing a book during that drive, as my education had been mostly technical. I can't say that literature was a passion of mine or that I read a lot of books. I guess spending hours on the road driving opens your mind to ideas. One of the company service representatives met me there to do the call. Her name was Donna.

Donna had long, wavy blond hair. She was slightly shorter than me and nicely trim, but not too thin. Her legs were well-toned and shapely. She filled out a professional suit perfectly, just enough butt, a nice bust line, and also had beautiful blue eyes. She was a few years younger than I was and single. We had traveled together on several sales and service calls.

Months before we had a company outing in Atlantic City, when Donald Trump had first opened his casino and the place was still up-and-coming. We toured the casino all evening together like husband and wife. She fell asleep on my shoulder on the bus that took us back to our hotel. I could tell I had feelings for her, but I kept reminding myself that I was a married man with a child in kindergarten. I kept reminding myself of how I'd screwed up early on in my marriage when I had been stationed in California for work. I thought of how humiliated I had felt when I realized Sonja had played me for sex. I had been so naive. In that bus, I just looked at that sleeping blond and swore, "No way, it's not going to happen again." I concentrated on how much I loved my wife and that I was going to live my life right. I should have realized then that I deserved to be divorced a long time ago. Luckily, it was several months before Donna and I saw each other again.

LIFE IN SALES

large companies like to own things. They buy buildings; they buy real estate; they acquire computer systems and software. But most of all, they like owning people. The way companies own people is by paying them large amounts of money. Once you get above a certain pay grade, the company basically owns you. They pretty much get to tell you when to jump and how high. For the sales staff, this meant travel.

I originally covered the New England territory for the California firm that employed me. That firm, an insurance company that provided products and services to banks and finance companies, was owned by a larger manufacturing company. The parent company was having a rough year and decided to do a reduction in force. Despite the insurance company subsidiary being very profitable, we, too, had to do a reduction, and I ended up covering Maine to Memphis. It was pretty much impossible to keep tabs on all the potential leads, effectively follow up, and therein close deals. I would instead get on a flight or take a train early Monday morning from Albany to New York City, where I'd meet with bankers at the largest banks in the city during the daytime and entertain them at night.

Bankers, who wore conservative navy blue or gray suits and white shirts with boring ties by day, liked to party like frat boys off my company's dime at night. The evenings often started at one of NYC's many expensive steak houses. It wasn't uncommon to drop $600 or $700 for dinner for four in the early 1990s. After dinner the nice bankers were all too ready to have me hand them a wad of twenties to use at midtown "gentlemen's clubs."

Hell, there was nothing gentlemanly about these clubs. They were titty bars, plain and simple. I never was a fan of these strip clubs that so enamored the banker crowd. To me it was akin to going for steak, ordering a fine filet mignon, having it brought to the table where you could look at it, smell it, and pay handsomely for it, but never eat it. What was the point? I could only imagine those bankers had wives at home who never let them see them undressed or something like that. Maybe it was a power thing, getting a young woman to spend more and more time shaking her breasts and ass in front of you because you tucked more and more money into her G-string. You could look, but you could never touch. Touching would get you tossed out in a New York second and you were lucky if you didn't get a twisted or broken arm to go with that ejection. The strip club bouncers were bad dudes. No, I never understood the attraction. It wasn't like any of these fat middle-aged bankers stuck around to closing and then took one of the young strippers to a hotel to have sex with her.

One night while out at a post-dinner titty bar with two bankers, a tall, slender blond dancer kept eyeing our booth. The place was crowded, so we were not at the bar where the patrons would stuff money in the girls' G-strings. The bankers had martinis but I had a Heineken as I had work to do back at my hotel, and I was trying to stay as sober as possible. At some point near the end of the set, the blond dancer pulled the money out of her G-string and finished the act totally nude. She slipped on a see-through robe and joined our booth. The three of us had just about finished our first round of drinks. As soon as the young dancer sat down, the waitress appeared to take more drink orders. The bankers each ordered another martini and I got another Heineken. Our tab for the first round was $29.50. I expected that, at $11.00 each for shelf-quality gin martinis and $7.50 for an import beer. The young dancer ordered a white Russian. The next tab was $69.50. I looked at the waitress and must have mumbled, "What the fuck?" a little too loudly. It wasn't twenty seconds before a large muscular bouncer was at our booth asking if there was a problem. We assured him there was no problem as he asked to settle up the entire tab, which somehow now was at $99 plus tip. I reached for my corporate American Express card, but I was quickly told, "Cash only." I only had about $45 on me and the bankers sat there as if they had never heard of this thing known as "cash." I asked the bouncer where the closest ATM was located. He gave me directions and proceeded to make me leave my entire wallet with the exception of my ATM card and driver's license with him. The two bankers were told to sit tight and enjoy the next set until I got back. I returned with $200 in cash and as I was calculating tip, I casually asked the dancer if she got a cut on her drink. At least she was honest enough to admit she did. I would have hoped she got the entire bottle of vodka for that money. She told us she had come to the USA from the Ukraine and was studying to become a doctor, a trauma surgeon specifically. I really hoped I would not come to an emergency room in Queens some day with this tall blond member of the itty-bitty titty club standing over me, saying, "You have bean in berry bad accident. You must have operation. I am Dr. Petrov and veel be doing your surgery. Vee vill take berry goot care of you."

After counting out $120, which covered the $99 for the bill and rounding up for the usual twenty percent tip, my clients and I started to leave, only to be stopped by the bouncer again. He came after us just short of the door and said we hadn't left enough money.

I looked at my bill again and said, "I left $99 for the drinks and a hair over the twenty percent for the tip. What's the problem?"

He informed me the minimum tip when sitting in a booth was $10 a person. This bastard was going to bleed me dry. I peeled off another $10 and asked if there were any more hidden charges. He said "Fuck off and get out before I throw your sorry asses out in the street."

Lots of New York City charm in those Midtown gentlemen's clubs.

Mondays, it was meetings by day in New York and fine dining in the evening, wine followed by martinis and boobs. Tuesdays were a train to Boston and repeat. Wednesdays were a flight to Pittsburg and replay the same shit, although the steaks weren't quite as expensive in Pittsburgh and sometimes the drink of choice was pitcher after pitcher of beer. Thursdays were for another city where I would wake up and have to look at the area code on the phone in the hotel to find out where I was that day. By Friday evenings, I would finally get to book a flight home, usually arriving around 10:30 pm. My flights were always first-class, though, as I was in the elite status on the prevalent carrier out of Albany.

Based on the amount of money the company was paying me, and the belief that among the executive team the sales person with the highest expense account would eventually sign the biggest clients, I was pretty much locked into a life leading to liver disease and obesity. I traveled every day, drank and ate too much, and never saw my wife or daughter except on weekends when I was too tired to be worth a shit. But hey, my base salary was pretty fat and the lure of the possible six-figure commission checks was constantly dangling in front of me. It was all worth it to give my family a better life.

Beth liked the money I was making, the new cars she drove and that we were financially comfortable. She also was completely focused on being a mom. It was as if she was making up for the years she had been a working mom and we when we had to have a baby sitter for Ann while she worked.

Ann really didn't know much of a different life. For as long as she could remember, her dad travelled during the week. She always looked forward to me bringing home small gifts for her when I traveled. I made it a point to buy her something if I was gone for more than three days in a row. Unfortunately, that was pretty much every week. She also looked forward to her dad grilling food on the weekend. Every now and then she got to go with me on the train to New York City for Take-Your-Daughter-To-Work Day. I have to admit, I felt like a failure as a father most of the time. Trinkets from the airport gift shop didn't make up for the lost time and not seeing your little girl grow up.

There was a little fun to all the business travel. I spent a lot of time on flights and I met some interesting people. One day, I was making a connection from Albany through Pittsburgh on the way to the home office in California. I was sitting alone in first class when Fred Rogers—yes, that Mr. Rogers—walked by me, heading into coach. I called the flight attendant over and said, "Mr. Rogers just got on and is sitting in coach. I want to upgrade him." Back in those days you used paper certificates to upgrade to first class. I pulled an upgrade certificate out of my large stash and handed it to her. She upgraded him to first class. Mr. Rogers gave me an autographed photo for my daughter. She was a little old for his show at that point, but I wasn't going to turn it down.

On a flight from LaGuardia to LAX, I was seated in first class as usual when two large fellows sat down in the first row in first class on the opposite side of the plane. There were only the three of us in first class. I immediately knew the one guy; was Larry Csonka, who had played running back for the undefeated 1972 Miami Dolphins. They were the only NFL team to have had a perfect season, winning every game and the Super Bowl. I also knew he grew up in Ohio near where I grew up and that my mother-in-law was best friends in high school with his aunt. It was a five-hour flight, so I waited about an hour before I got up and asked him "Hey, didn't you play for the Stow, Ohio Bulldogs?"

Csonka was a bit dumbfounded. He laughed and told me that yes, he had played for the Stow Bulldogs. I sat down across from him and gave him the story about the connection between his aunt and my mother-in-law. I pulled out one of my business cards and asked for an autograph, which he happily gave me. I was about to have a major mental lapse and say, "Thanks Mr. Butkus," naming a player who had played for the Chicago Bears. Butkus had been a monster defensive player, Csonka, an offensive running back. Luckily my mouth stopped working and my brain re-engaged before the slip came out.

I met a lot of other people on my flights. I was also lucky to meet a few big-name politicians and other famous people. I'd met a few minor rock 'n' roll celebrities, too; one I particularly remember—Stephen Bishop—who had some success with his songs "On & On" and "Save It For a Rainy Day." He was a very down-to-earth guy who acted just like any other passenger on a flight. We shot the shit all the way from Pittsburgh to LA. He could have been my next-door neighbor.

I also remember a late-night connection in Pittsburg into Albany. I was coming out of Los Angeles and was dead tired. I'd been in a meeting all day and it was late. I'd missed lunch and the flight before had not served a meal. I was again the only person in first class. When the flight attendant came around with the snack basket, I asked to grab a few extras, as I hadn't eaten all day. I had a good glass of wine to go with my pretzels and cookies, thinking that would have to constitute dinner for the day. The flight attendant came back in a few minutes with a filet mignon steak dinner complete with a baked potato and salad. I was shocked. He said it had been left over from their last leg and was going to get thrown away. I know it was airline food, but back in the day first class food wasn't too bad, and that night I could have been at the best chophouse in New York City. The steak was divine. I got the flight attendant's name and drafted a letter on my laptop to the president of the airlines who conveniently was listed inside the in-flight magazine. I praised the flight attendant for saving me that night. I hope he got some notation in his work record for the letter.

SERVICE CALLS

Among the sales calls, fine dining, excessive drinking, and strip clubs, I would get to do service calls to existing accounts. In retrospect, maybe liver disease and obesity in exchange for just doing sales calls wouldn't have been so bad. The accounts I called on for sales were deals that ranged anywhere from ten million over three years to as high as fifty million over a three-year deal. My commission on that kind of money was huge.

Doing service calls, on the other hand, were done just to ensure that the client knew who we were so when bidding time for the next contract came up, they were comfortable with our sales team as much as they were with operations.

Fucking service. There was that blond again. Donna always seemed to show up on the service calls to which I was assigned. In a way, service calls were a reprieve from the grind of sales. You went to accounts that were already under contract. Our contracts were three years long with our clients. Generally, the sales people stayed involved when a client first came on board during the transition from the previous vendor and during the life of the existing contract. Our business wasn't very sexy. We tracked insurance required by lenders on property, homes, or commercial buildings and vehicles. If the borrower didn't maintain the insurance the lender required, we notified the borrower via a few letters. If borrowers didn't send in the proof of the insurance to us, we placed an insurance policy on the borrower and then the lender billed the borrower for the premium. Unfortunately, our firm took the calls from the borrowers who got the letters notifying them of their lapse of insurance and of the premiums they were being charged. Suffice to say they weren't a happy bunch of callers. No matter if these borrowers had not done anything required of them; once they got charged the premium and their loan payment went up, they were destined to call their local bank branch and complain about the "insurance department," which is what we generically called ourselves as well. Our service team made nice with the bankers, ensuring them that we were treating their rudest customers with utmost respect and care.

I had signed a medium-sized bank on Long Island and we were getting into the implementation process when I met Donna. Donna was pretty, but not more so than my wife. She also had a sense of confidence about her that most women didn't have. It wasn't arrogance, but she could hold her own when things got heated with a client. She wasn't argumentative, but she could firmly express her position while still making the clients feel like they were somehow winning the battle. At the end of the discussion, she always got her way and yet the clients felt like it had been their idea all along.

Donna and I had a meeting with a bank on Long Island and had wrapped up for the day. We were driving back to Manhattan, where she was to accompany me on a sales call the next day. As she sat in the passenger seat, she got out a little container of breath mints and popped one in her mouth. She asked if I wanted one, but I knew she was joking because she had taken the last one.

I pulled up to a red light and sarcastically I said, "Yes, the one in your mouth." She leaned over in the car and kissed me deeply, slipping the mint into my mouth in the process. The light changed, and I drove on into the city somewhat stunned. There was no conversation. I really hadn't known what to say at that point except, "Thank you."

When we got to our hotel near Grand Central Station, we took the elevator up to the thirtieth floor where her room was located. I was carrying her suitcase. We went into her room and I sat down on the bed. She simply knelt down in front of me, undid my belt, unzipped my pants, and began giving me oral sex. She didn't ask if she could, and I didn't stop her. My mind was screaming, "NO, YOU'RE A MARRIED MAN!" but the rest of me wasn't paying any attention.

She was skilled. She knew all the right techniques to drive a man right to the edge of orgasm and then back off just enough to keep him pleading for more. You don't think about where a woman learns so much about giving such good oral sex when you are receiving it. You do start to think about it later.

I regained my senses and had her stop short of finishing the experience. I said we'd talk about it all at dinner. I left her room and got to my room, cursing myself for letting myself get into such a situation. I thought back to the incident with Sonja and how stupid I had felt for not being stronger and saying "no." How I let my wife down and now I'd done it again. Yet there I had been with another woman's mouth all over my junk. What the hell had happened?

We decided upon a quiet Italian restaurant that had been recommended by a friend of mine who lived in the city. The restaurant wasn't in a touristy part of town. It was in a place where the people who actually live in NYC went to eat. It was a quaint little place, and when we walked in, the waitress immediately mistook us for husband and wife. We didn't do anything to correct her.

I ordered a glass of wine, but Donna declined one. I was perplexed. We talked for a few minutes and then Donna confessed, "I'm a recovering alcoholic. Five years sober now."

"I guess that explains the evening in Atlantic City where you never ordered a cocktail," I replied. It put me a little on edge as I was used to a martini before dinner, a few glasses of wine over dinner, and then a sherry or port after dinner. "I guess skipping the martini and just having one glass of wine would be a lot healthier for me anyhow."

We discussed the kiss in the car. She said, "I've wanted to kiss you for a long time, ever since the first time I saw you in the office. You turned me on the day I met you. Traveling with you made it even worse. I knew it was only a matter of time before you'd be in my bed."

She knew I was married. I'd shown her pictures of my wife and daughter many times. It wasn't like I had been leading her on; at least I thought I hadn't. I couldn't think of anything I'd done to suggest I was open to a relationship. Maybe I was being naive again. Maybe this was my brother's years of throwing his sexual prowess into my face I was trying to overcome. On the surface I knew I didn't want to hurt my wife. I loved Beth. But in front of me was a very beautiful woman who was initiating sex, something my wife rarely did these days. I was so confused. I knew what I should be doing, and yet I seemed to be unable to resist the excitement of doing it anyhow.

I was flattered as not many women tell guys who had been married over ten years that they are attracted to them, that they are handsome and want to have sex with them. I was in pretty good physical condition as I did manage to hit the workout facilities at the hotels as much as possible. I still had some pretty good blond hair and a young-looking face for thirty-six. That face worked against me in my sales call with the much older bankers. At first glance, they saw a face of inexperience. It wasn't until I had met with the older bankers a few times that they began to see that I had a keen understanding of their business needs and that I came up with unique, yet implementable solutions. But the future of my life hinged on what happened next. If I was going to be a faithful husband, I had to know why I hadn't stopped what happened at the hotel. I tried to think of a graceful way to ask about the oral sex, but there just isn't a way to ask, "And so why did you give me a blow job?" I let it go.

As we got back to the hotel, we stopped at Donna's hotel room. I knew I was standing at the gates of hell and sexual pleasure at the same time. "Conflicted" couldn't even begin to describe my feelings. She asked me in to talk about planning the next day's calls. OK, I thought, we're back to business mode. I could do this.

The hotel room was small, so I sat down on the bed again. I took off my jacket, opened my briefcase. Donna had gone to the bathroom to freshen up, and I heard the sound of her electric toothbrush followed by the flush of a toilet. And then she came out wearing nothing but a short silk robe. She looked at me squarely in the eyes and asked, "How far off this cliff do you want to jump?"

I sat perplexed by what she had said for what seemed like a very long time, and it hit me that I was in a circular argument. Once you step off the cliff, you are already all the way off. It isn't like you only step halfway off…and at that point I realized I had already cheated on my wife. The moment I had let her go down on me, I was falling off the cliff. It wasn't a partial step. It was an all-or-none choice and I didn't have the courage to say "no."

I guess I wanted the attention of another beautiful woman. And here she was, and my wife was 185 miles away. Donna simply pushed me back on the bed and slowly undressed me. She went back to giving me oral sex, at which she was very skilled, knowing just when and how to flick her tongue, when to work the strokes and when to bury it deep in her mouth. She could also determine when I was getting close to climax. Clearly, she wanted that for a different reason. She pushed me back on the bed, dropped her robe to reveal her fully nude body, and lay down beside me. It was my turn to demonstrate my skills at oral sex. I don't know how long I was down on her, but I do know she gently guided my fingers up her ass as I was busy working to bring her to climax. I got her to climax and sat up before mounting her for my finish. One thing I noticed was her breasts had fallen completely off the side of her body as if deflated. In retrospect a lot of her body looked like it had been deflated. I wasn't distracted, though, and got right to work on a vigorous screw. She enjoyed twisting her nipples during sex, which I'd never seen a woman do, and she was really into having my fingers in her ass as we fucked.

When we finished, I rolled off her and she simply asked, "Are you OK?"

I really wasn't sure of my answer. I had just broken the most sacred vow you make to your spouse, but I had never been fucked so well in my life. The mental conflict was anguishing.

Luckily for me Donna had a flight back to the California headquarters after the early morning sales meeting the next day. There wouldn't be much time to talk about had what happened between us. I needed time to process it all. Was there any way to un-jump off that cliff? I guessed that if I kept my mouth shut, there really wouldn't be any way for Beth to find out. I told myself that I must act normal and forget my time with Donna. It had been a mistake and I wouldn't let it happen again. That was my plan.

I got back home and Beth was frazzled by a tough week at work and from taking care of Ann entirely by herself.

"Kevin, I have been eating macaroni and cheese for dinner all week. It's all Ann would eat. I want to go out to dinner," Beth pleaded.

"Beth, I have had to look at a damn menu every meal all week. The last thing I want is to go to another restaurant," I groaned.

"OK, honey. What can I make for you?"

"Damnit, I don't know. Think of something. I am sick and tired of having to decide every meal. Just make me something," I bitched back at her.

It wasn't what she was looking for. She wanted adult conversation, adult company. I think she just wanted to have a normal evening with her husband. Secretly, I was feeling pretty pleased with myself. I had a beautiful blond providing me sex at a hotel and a wife at home wanting to serve my domestic needs. That feeling of terror that I'd felt at the hotel after the sexual encounter had passed and I was feeling like I pretty much had it made.

"OK, can you just bake a chicken breast while I take a shower?" I finally told Beth. She should have kicked me in the balls and thrown me out the door right there.

I was excited for the coming weekend. It was time to replace my old company car, as they had switched to a higher allowance. I knew I had a lot of leeway in the car I could choose. Most of my counterparts across the country drove low-end Cadillacs or high-end Buicks with a Lincoln thrown in now and then. I was a little different. I had to navigate tight city streets if I drove to NYC, Boston, or Providence. I wanted something classy. Something a little smaller, yet something that made a statement.

Like a new 1994 BMW 318i, black of course. It was a four-door sedan as required under company rules. I picked it up from the dealer with about every option you could buy on the car except with a five-speed manual. There were no rules that said the company car had to be an automatic.

The first time my regional VP rode in the BMW with me, he flipped out a bit when he saw the size; he drove a huge Cadillac and really freaked at the sight of a five-speed stick shift. We drove through the streets of New York City and Boston and he quit his pissing and moaning. I think he began to understand why the smaller BMW was a better fit for the tight streets of big cities. Hell, if I'd really had my way, I would be driving a BMW Z3 3.2L M Series, a two-seater convertible that would go zero to sixty in 5.1 seconds. I liked pushing the boundaries.

Life at home on the weekends was pretty good. I had a loving wife, a cute little daughter, and a big, friendly golden retriever, Buddy. We had gotten Buddy from a farm in Massachusetts. He had been a terror as a puppy but had grown up to be a loveable, big lug. He was a great dog that we took with us everywhere on the weekends. Beth had a Jeep Cherokee four-wheel drive that was very safe in the New York winters. We'd go around in the Jeep or the BMW as the happy little family unit, mom, dad, the cute little daughter, Buddy the golden retriever tooling around Saratoga Springs.

To the neighbors we must have looked like the all-American, success-story family. Beth did lament about the long business trips that took me away from home, but her friends envied the expensive vacations we took. As I had tons of airline and hotel points, we always flew first class to nice destinations and stayed in first-class hotels on the best beaches. Since we only had one child, we most always took one of Ann's friends with us to keep her company. Mostly the other parents were jealous that their kid was going on a vacation that they themselves couldn't afford. Our friends in the neighborhood took family vacations similar to what I took as a kid, everyone packed in the car driving to a cabin in Canada or maybe in Maine. Saratoga Springs, while it had some old money as evidence by the stately mansions around the historic downtown area, mostly had become a sprawl of suburbs for middle-class people struggling to make ends meet.

We ended up being far better off than any of our neighbors, and they knew it. We weren't warmly welcomed into the neighborhood by all. During August we would go to the racetrack and bet a little on the horses. We never bet big and therefore never lost or won big, either. Winters were for downhill skiing, including the mountains where they had the 1980 Winter Olympics.

Beth often complained about the winters. She wasn't a skier, and Ann was too small for anything except bunny slopes. As such, I spent time skiing alone. But there were some special moments up there in the frigid winters. My family stood on the famed ice rink where the rag-tag USA hockey team beat the mighty Soviets in hockey on the way to win the gold medal. We all tried cross-country skiing. I skied Whiteface Mountain on the same course the Olympic downhill course had been. I even broke my thumb on it. I carried a secret love for the winters.

When I wasn't traveling on business, I worked from home. An unwritten rule in the world of large-scale business-to-business sales is you never make a call to anyone after noon on a Friday. People are trying to wrap up their week and talking to a salesperson is killing valuable time they need to maybe sneak out a little early. As such, good salespeople saved their call reports and other paperwork for Friday afternoons. Since I was on the leading edge of using computers in the sales force, I had my reports done early and was usually able to take off for an afternoon of skiing in the winter or golf in the summer on Fridays.

The mountains were a short drive away and the views were wonderful. The crowds of the weekend had not carved up the ski slopes yet, so I mostly had virgin snow. I often had runs all to myself. The combination of the glistening afternoon sun, frosted pines, and pristine snow-covered runs was a sight to behold. While we didn't have the powder snow like the Rockies, we had the faster snow

Olympic racers crave. I had skied some slopes in Northern Ohio as a teen, but those slopes were tiny in comparison to those in New York and Vermont. I never had lessons other than tips from fellow, more experienced skiers. While living in New York, I learned over time how to hold an edge in ice, how to flatten my skis to gain speed, and how to cut a sharp turn to avoid a tree.

The skies in upstate New York and in Vermont were generally crystal blue unless a snowstorm was coming down. Putting those skies as a backdrop to the evergreen pines and the brilliant white snow was a picture I'll never forget.

My solitary skiing also gave me time to think and reflect on what I was doing with my life. I was not knocking sales out of the park. I was making respectable money, but was it worth being away so much from my family? And there was my infidelity. Why did I keep doing the same stupid thing that I knew was wrong over and over again? I couldn't even come up with an answer for myself. Maybe I should have missed one of those turns on the slope and hit a big tree. Perhaps it would have knocked some sense into me.

I should have been a happier man, but something was burning inside of me. Damn that woman. Beth was beginning to see a change in me. I'd fallen off the cliff and was continuing to free-fall with no bottom in sight. Why had I gotten involved with Donna? My conscience was ripping me up inside. Deep down I wanted to be the faithful husband Beth wanted me to be, to be the person I wanted me to be, but why was I failing over and over again? It was as if there was some switch in my brain that was turned off at the wrong moments, and I didn't know how to keep it turned on. I knew immediately afterward that what I'd done was wrong, but at the moment I seemed unable to stop myself from letting stupid things from happening. I was smarter than this. I knew better than this. But why couldn't I stop myself?

I arranged a sales call to an account in Cleveland knowing Donna was to be in town. I told my boss that I was going to go over to visit a client who was in town for a Browns game. Donna and I agreed to spend the night at her hotel. We ordered room service and watched Monday Night Football for a while. At some point I turned the game off and turned to her, saying, "Donna, where is this going?"

"Where is what going, honey?"

"Us? This whole thing? We've been seeing each other, and trust me I am really enjoying the sex. But I need to know what this is."

"Why can't you just enjoy yourself?" she replied.

"I have consequences. I am married with a kid. You are completely unattached. I understand why I was attracted to you. Damn, you are beautiful. But please, I have to have something. I have to know if there is something behind those wonderful blue eyes. Do you have feelings for me, or is this just for fun for you?" I pleaded.

"Why do you have to make this into something? When you are home, you are a husband and a father. You're with HER!" she said harshly. "When you are away, you are sometimes with me and we have fun. What's wrong with that? You aren't taking time away from your family to be with me. You aren't supporting me. You aren't buying me expensive gifts. All I want is your attention when I have you to myself."

She definitely felt justified.

I wasn't sure how to respond. I gently stroked her thick, blond hair and looked into those limpid blue eyes that seemed suddenly to be welling up a bit with tears. I hugged her closely and let the conversation go. I turned the football game back on and pulled her close to me under the thick comforter on the king-sized bed. I gazed out the window high above the Cleveland skyline.

"I've always loved the sound of Al Michaels' voice you

know," she said.

"What? Al Michaels?"

"He's calling the game. He has a very sexy voice," she purred.

I really didn't know what to think or say.

CALIFORNIA

Quarterly all the sales team were called into the corporate office in Irvine, California for sales meetings. The meetings each lasted a week. They were a combination of training, team building, and socializing. I had three counterparts spread around the country. Donna wasn't in sales, but the service people would be involved in the entire meeting. She and I had been having a series of phone and email conversations since the NYC trip, but they had been playful. I really did not expect anything to happen on my next trip out to the home office. I had my first account up and running that was producing a reasonable degree of income for the firm, and I was working hard to ensure several of the largest banks in NYC and Boston had us in their sights as the number one possibility when their contracts came up with their current vendors. My boss knew how hard I'd been working, and his boss knew it as well. They liked the relationships I was building with our key prospects. They didn't know about the relationship I was building with the blond service representative who was just down the hall from them.

My first night at the hotel, I got a knock on my door late in the evening. I was expecting the hotel turndown service. Instead, it was Donna with an over-sized tote bag. She invited herself in and said, "Are you up for a night of fun?"

Once again, I found my big head telling the little head that this was not a good idea. That no matter how good the sex was, it was not worth hurting my wife over. And then she pulled out the butt beads. I had no idea what they were for, but she was about to teach me. She was very into anal stimulation. Here I was, 2,800 miles from home, four time zones away, with a hot woman in my room, naked wanting me to have sex with her. This was so far out of my reality; I had no clue how to process it. So I caved.

Afterward Donna turned and looked at me and said "Now wasn't that good? I have so much to teach you."

What could I say except that, yeah, it had been damn good. I kept trying to tell myself that I was not taking anything away from my family. I would have been 2,800 miles away that night even if I hadn't screwed her. I didn't spend any money on her. The only thing I'd given up was a few ounces of semen. And maybe also my wilting confidence that I would ever be a faithful husband to a great wife.

I kept telling myself I wasn't taking anything away from my family. Still, I was really feeling like a crap weasel. It is funny how you can begin to fool yourself if you tell yourself the same lie over and over. You actually begin to believe the lie yourself.

Each night that week I was in California, after the corporate dinners were over, Donna and I would end up together either at my hotel or at her apartment. One night, she stayed until morning at my hotel, which was a bit risky as the other sales reps from out of town were also at the same hotel. That morning as she was putting on her make-up, which she always did in the nude, I was trying to comb my hair behind her.

"Honey, I have something special for you," Donna softly said.

I was surprised when she reached back with her left hand and began stroking me. I got hard in seconds. As she was putting make-up on with her right hand, she guided me into her bum as she slightly bent forward. I guess I had lived a bit of a sexually sheltered life because up to that point I had never had anal sex.

"I'll bet you've never tried this before, have you?" she asked as she pushed back onto me, pushing me deeper into her.

It became obvious she had done this many times before. Perhaps it was the excitement of doing something so wrong that kept me coming back. Maybe secretly I wanted to be more of the "bad boy" like my brother was who could casually screw women and feel nothing. She just smiled and continued to put on make-up. I also thought this was surreal. Why would a woman this good-looking give herself so willingly to me so often? My wife didn't offer sex at every moment we were together. What was going on? I was having serious issues processing what was happening. I was having real confusion distinguishing sexual passion from actual loving emotions, and it was going to be trouble. It was one thing when this was casual sex, but when I started feeling emotions for Donna, I knew this was going the wrong direction. I think she had me where she wanted me. By now she knew I wouldn't say no to anything she requested. I finished with a simple "Thank you."

PLAYING ROLES

S ales people play roles all day long. Even at home I was playing the role of a faithful and happy husband. It wasn't like my life at home wasn't happy, but I was hiding a deep, dark secret. I chose to play the role of a happily married man.

I didn't get into sales by choice. I had lost a job and a sales position was the only thing on the table to pay the bills at the time. I had talked with dozens of salespeople at conferences that told the same story. They had been in another role, and they had lost their job. A sales job had opened up, and they had taken it. At the time I started in sales there were only three or four undergraduate degrees in business with a focus on sales offered in the United States, so very few people graduated from college intending to become a salesperson. Salespeople learn to act like the prospective buyer's best friend for months or maybe years on end in hopes it will score them a huge contract and therein commission. They eat with the prospective client; they take them to dinner, to strip clubs, to play golf, and, in my case, to the racetrack in Saratoga as well as skiing in Vermont. Salespeople did what they had to do to get the sale closed.

Some of the people I met with, I genuinely grew to like. There was a guy at a large NYC bank on 47th and Madison. Skip was in his late thirties and in a middle management position in the bank's insurance department. He wasn't going to be the final decision maker on the contract I offered to him in the next twenty-four months, but I was going to have to get Skip's approval to get my contract up the next rung of the bank's corporate ladder. Unlike most of the bankers I knew, Skip did not partake in the titty bar scene, which I respected. He showed more respect for both the vendors and the women at the gentlemen's clubs than most of his counterparts. He would mostly want to meet for lunch and an occasional dinner. He was one of the few guys I didn't have to role play in front of on every visit.

Each year on Take-Your-Daughter-To-Work Day, I'd arrange a meeting with Skip at his office and take Ann, who was in preschool, on the train from Albany to NYC. We would have a "business lunch" with Skip making it sound like we were talking about something important for a few minutes. It was a bit of a show for my little girl. After lunch Skip headed back to his job and Ann and I went to a large NYC toy store and go shopping. As messed up as things were in my life at the time, my trips to NYC with Ann were some of my best memories. I had this little rudder named Ann who was trying to keep my boat going straight. She had no idea she was doing it, but she was.

We were lucky to have conceived her. Beth's illness, which had caused her hospitalization when we met, made her getting pregnant questionable. She was on some pretty nasty medications for a long period afterward. When Ann was born with no defects, it was truly a blessing. I am not a spiritual person. But I do have a strong belief in a singular higher power, and I thanked him that day for my baby girl. Getting to participate, even as limited as it was, in her upbringing was the most special thing in my life. There is no stronger love a person can feel but for that of one's child, and I was fortunate to know that.

Ann was a very intelligent little girl. By the time she was in kindergarten she was reading at a second-grade level. Being an only-child, she always interacted well with adults. Ann was also a very cute kid. She got really lucky and got her mom's killer blue eyes and my blond hair.

Since she and I had always made it a point to spend time together each week, just her and I, we had a close bond. Even when she was a young kid, we talked about very mature subjects. The death of her grandmother, Beth's mom, was handled in a loving and considerate conversation. She understood how her grandma had been aging and failing in health. While she grieved her loss, she seemed to understand the process in a manner far more mature than I would have considered normal at her age of nine at the time.

Ann helped me see the value in our family unit. When I was making my mistakes, my thoughts often went back to her and what would happen if Beth divorced me and I would hardly see Ann at all. It didn't get my head in the right place all at once, but it had an effect on me.

Still, it was easy to begin to see flaws in my wife. Every time I asked to make love and Beth said "no," I secretly compared her to Donna, who was doing erotic things to me that my wife had never even thought of. It wasn't as if I was into erotic sex, but Donna constantly surprised me with unusual positions or new toys to try out when we were together. No, I married a decent woman who had only been with one man, me. I'd been happy with our sex life until Donna came along. I had regretted the mistake I made with Sonja. It was a foolish mistake and I regretted it terribly, but here I was throwing our life together into the trash again.

The role-playing on sales calls was getting more extreme as the company expanded my territory thanks to a layoff at the parent company. When I was first hired, I was only covering the New England region. Now I was covering Maine to Memphis. I was under pressure to sign contracts of any size while I waited on the big guys in NYC and Boston to come around to putting out their requests for proposals. That meant calling on some smaller and mid-sized institutions. Some lenders were fine, but others got the idea they should get the same entertainment treatment as the top banks in the country.

I had a mortgage company in Buffalo, NY whose reps I had met with during the day and had agreed to take out to dinner that evening. It was a mixed group of men and women. I had gotten into Buffalo mid-day and gone straight into meetings with people from their insurance, lending, operations, and technology departments. It consumed my entire afternoon. I barely had time to drop my bag in my hotel room and make my way to the restaurant where they were already eager to start drinking and eating on my company's nickel.

After several hours of martinis, steaks, wine, and finally dessert, I thought we'd reached the end of the night. Oh, I was so wrong. The executive vice president who controlled which company would be awarded the next contact was a woman of about fifty. She was very drunk.

She also thought I was a boy toy sent there for her pleasure. She had been uncomfortably flirting with me all evening and had been putting her hand on my leg under the table throughout dinner. This is where salespeople are put in a very difficult position, particularly at this time in the mid-1990s. There were no guidelines on what you did in these cases. A lot depended on how big the client or prospect was. Sad to say, but the bigger the contract, the more crap they usually could get away with doing—and they knew it.

When dessert was served, the female VP started by putting whipped cream on her finger and telling me to lick it off. Most everyone at the table—well, mainly her staff— laughed. Our operations manager, Frank, who was sitting across from me, looked sick to his stomach. OK, it was a pretty good-sized prospect, so what the hell, I licked it off. Next, she put some whipped cream on her nose and demanded the same. I complied. I had had at least five martinis and six glasses of wine with dinner. At this time, the adage in sales was that if the client drinks, you drink, and if the client smokes a cigar, you smoke a cigar. I was not in any shape to make rational decisions, and she knew it. But what she did next turned my stomach for years. She stuck her tongue into the whipped cream and pulled my face over to her, making me suck it off her tongue. It was about the lowest point of my business career. I was being used as this woman's sex toy because she knew I could not say "no." Saying "no" would mean our company got scratched from the list of potential vendors for the next contract. She was the one who held the power.

The group dropped me off at my hotel. I had no idea what room I was in or if I was even at the right hotel. In slurred words I explained my dilemma to the hotel staff and gave them my driver's license. I couldn't have thanked the two guys working the front desk enough for getting me to my room. I got up in time to catch a flight to the next city on my itinerary the next day. I was sick to my stomach— not from the booze, but from the thought of how I had been molested. I had a small sense of what a woman must feel like when she has been raped. I felt dirty and somehow it was my fault. My "molestation" unfortunately happened in front of prospective clients and our operations manager from our Pittsburgh office, Frank. I didn't know how I would ever face Frank in a meeting again.

Life was spinning out of control. We eventually did land the account and thankfully the vice president retired. I could never have faced her again, drunk or sober. I don't know if the incident of her sticking her whipped cream-covered tongue down my throat had anything to do with her retirement, but who knows, maybe karma is a bitch and for that vice president, she had come around. I wondered how long it would be before karma had something in store for me messing around on my wife.

In addition to taking on the largest physical territory in the country, I took on a new role in our company's sales department. Because of my technology background, I had been chosen to help select and roll out a personal computer platform to everyone on the sales team. I was the only salesperson at the time using a laptop computer to track my calls, write reports, and check emails remotely. The executive over the sales area decided that all of the sales team needed to start using the same tools. As such I was called in to spend a lot of time in the home office.

Being at the home office meant being around Donna daily. We did a good job of maintaining a professional appearance while at the office; at least we thought we did. Evenings were a different story. There was no sales team at the hotel to possibly run into, so she was in my room almost every night. My direct manager wanted me to stay over the weekend every other weekend to save on the travel budget. I put up a feigned fight but agreed to do so for the "good of the company." Fuck the company. I was just looking forward to spending time with Donna. I started spending the night at her apartment and things started to get a lot clearer.

Beth wasn't happy about the every-other-weekend travel, but it wasn't entirely different than what I did during the conference season. I'd leave home on a Saturday to be at a convention center first thing Sunday to begin setting up our display booth for the conference that started Sunday evening. It wasn't uncommon for me to go directly on sales calls until Friday after the conference ended Wednesday. I was always gone a lot. She didn't like it, but it was what our life had been for many years.

There was constant sex when I was in California. Every

evening, after a comforting call to my wife and daughter in NY, it was dinner with Donna and something new to be explored. She was into everything. I was not into S&M or bondage stuff, so she let that go.

It was all fun and games until one night when she asked me to go to a place I was not comfortable. Donna had told me she was a recovering alcoholic and went to twelve-step meetings regularly. What she wanted to do one evening was unusual compared to a NYC kinky club setting and even more bizarre for someone who was in AA. She had me strip down and lay on her bed, whereupon she started giving me fantastic oral sex. Part of the way through, she stopped and carefully dried my junk with a towel. She went to her dresser and got out a small vile of white powder and a straw. She had me lay still while she poured a line of coke down my junk and snorted it.

I wasn't into cocaine. I'd tried it years before in college before meeting my wife, and frankly, that shit scared the hell out of me. I was convinced anything that made me feel that good would make me an addict in an instant. I'd seen how easily my brother was addicted to alcohol and drugs and they scared me. He'd had the opportunity to get a full-ride scholarship to at least a mid-sized college for football, but his addiction to alcohol and drugs left him a high-school dropout working menial jobs with no future.

Donna shook her head back, laughed, and proceeded to mount and ride me wildly. I don't know who came first or how many times. I know I was spent way before she was, in any case.

We were both covered in sweat, lying nude next to each other. Her wild rage of sex had calmed. I had developed feelings for her and was terrified by what I'd witnessed. The sun was setting low in the California sky, just barely peeking into her apartment window a few blocks off the beach. She looked beautiful as the sun glistened off the sweat on her body. She was totally comfortable nude, something Beth never was. I asked how she reconciled being a recovering alcoholic with doing coke.

Donna looked deeply into my eyes and said, "Alcohol was used against me by my ex-husband to get me drunk and fat. I was almost one hundred pounds heavier at one point. He used it to make me complicit to his demands of his sexual fantasies that included me having sex with multiple men at one. It allowed me to endure gang bangs and to be raped with objects. Once I was drunk, I'd get passed around for his friends to screw at parties. After a while I learned to stay drunk to numb the abuse. It wasn't until I met another woman who was in AA that I began my recovery."

Donna said she told this woman about her sexual abuse, and the woman convinced her to come to a women's-only meeting. She began to draw courage from the group to divorce her husband. After the divorce and sobriety, she discovered she missed some of the sexual activity and began exploring things back on her own terms. I was seeing the things she enjoyed, not what was forced on her.

Donna added, "Cocaine isn't a habit. It is something I use occasionally to enhance the sexual experiences I choose to have."

I sat there with tears in my eyes. This woman was really messed up. I wasn't sure I was buying all of it, but I am sure she had a very bad past. Someone had really abused her on many levels. Her "deflated" breasts and loose skin were evidence of her extreme weight loss. At this moment, I thought back to our various encounters and what I did begin to see was a pattern of how we had sex. She would always initiate it after she had been alone for a few moments. I had assumed she would take that time to "freshen up" or go to the bathroom. In reality, she had been doing a line of coke.

The only time this wasn't the case was when we had sex when we first woke up, which was always soft and gentle.

There were never any toys or exotic acts, just simple cuddling followed by tender sex. Those mornings may have been the only times I'd had pure sex with Donna. The rest was cocaine-fueled rage sex somehow designed as payback against her ex-husband, or maybe against all men.

There was no doubt in my mind at this point that I was being used. I thought I had feelings for her and that my wife was somehow failing me. It is so easy to mistake the emotions you feel when you are having sex for love. But sex is just a physical act. Love is something that someone does twenty-four hours a day, seven days a week, fifty-two weeks a year. They love you when you are there, when you are away, when you are sick—all the time. Donna was only having sex with me. I'd been so wrong. I was a sexual marionette that Donna could pull out of the box when she wanted, pull the strings she wanted, and get exactly the response she desired. When she was done fucking me, or more accurately not fucking her ex-husband or whomever he demanded of her, she sent me away and didn't have to worry about me.

I could not discuss the affair with any co-workers. I could not discuss it with my wife. I was very much alone. I thought I was being loved. Instead, I was being owned by yet another entity, and this one owned my cock and balls. Worst of all, she was leading me to believe that it was Beth who was failing me. She constantly told me if Beth loved me, she would have more sex with me; if Beth loved me more, she would perform this or do that. Donna was planting seeds routinely that it was Beth who was failing as a wife for not fulfilling my sexual needs.

I have no idea if Donna wanted me to be with her full-time or if she was just hell-bent to destroy my marriage for some crazy reason. Maybe Donna wanted what Beth had, someone who crawled into bed with her every night and put his arm around her as they fell asleep. Beth often complained as I snuggled to her at night that I kept her awake. Maybe that is what attracted me to Donna. When we slept together, she pulled her body close to mine for the entire night. She moved my hands to her breasts at night while Beth pushed them away. She even took her clothes off during the night, saying my body radiated heat and kept her warm. Waking to a nude lover was an incredible sensation. I suppose Beth had gone through the "romance" period. She had done the snuggling and playful stuff. She had landed the husband, and in our Midwest culture, once you said "I do" at the altar, everything was done and over. No one cheated; no one broke his or her vows. She never anticipated another woman coming on to her husband and whispering sweet things into his ear, offering her body every time they were near each other. It wasn't fair to Beth. She had no clue what the big, bad world was shooting at her. To top it off, it was shooting all of this at a husband who had a weakness for sex.

Donna and I never really talked about what would happen if I left Beth. I guess I boldly assumed she would want to marry me. After all, two of the three women I'd had sex with had wanted to marry me. I was pretty self-confident on this issue, foolishly. I thought Donna would want to marry me as well. That would mean moving to the West Coast and almost never seeing my little Ann. I was at Donna's apartment when this reality hit me. She said Beth would start using Ann against me in the divorce negotiations. I started to cry. I'm not sure if it was because I was facing losing Ann and Beth or if I was seeing that Donna was truly controlling me. I needed a drink. But shit, she had nothing in the apartment.

ESCAPE

I had not seen Donna for about two weeks. I had been on the road since Monday and would be finishing the week in California, working a conference near our home office in Irvine, California. I still felt enslaved to the little tuft of blond pubic hair Donna maintained. She was either a true blond or worked really hard at keeping the curtains matching the carpet. I never knew for certain. Regardless, Donna was working the conference as well. Several of the sales reps were in town, so the times Donna and I were able to spend the night together were limited. During the daytime of a conference, the sales reps manned a booth on the vendor's display floor to talk to potential clients. In the evening, we had prearranged dinners with conference attendees, most of whom were current clients or hot prospects.

One night, the sales team was debating on whom to ask to fill one vacancy for a dinner due to a cancellation. We voted to invite a guy from my region. He worked for a mid-sized bank, which really was not a particularly good prospect. The guy was also a previous New York state insurance department regulator.

We went to The Palm in Beverly Hills. It was an expensive restaurant, as most are in Beverly Hills, but The Palm is on the higher end. We had a pretty good turnout for the dinner of about twenty people including myself, Donna, the senior VP over sales, and other prospects and clients. Ralph was the odd man out. No one really wanted an ex-insurance commissioner there. Bankers hated them. Regulators did nothing but make life difficult for the bank's insurance departments. The insurance companies like I worked for hated them, as they were just an obstacle to achieving our goals. They were under-achieving paper pushers who had to be bought off in ways that skirted federal and state laws. And these bastards knew it as well. They expected their palms to be greased. Now that Ralph was working for a bank, he still thought like a regulator and still thought everyone was supposed to grease his palm.

The Palm was a steak house where celebrities were frequently spotted. The walls were covered in rich walnut paneling and the carpet was a deep burgundy. Every inch of the place looked of money. There was nothing casual about it. It was where serious diners went. Big business deals were sealed over expensive bottles of champagne in this restaurant. The wait staff all looked to have years of experience. There were no starving artists working here. They were all well-compensated professionals.

Drink orders were taken. Donna, as usual, ordered a sparkling water, keeping up the AA image. I ordered my usual martini. Bottles of wine were ordered. Ralph managed to order the most expensive bourbon they had in stock. I had no idea he had ordered it until I saw the bill. Dinner orders were taken. Most prospects and clients were more than happy to abuse the vendor's credit card a bit, but Ralph—oh, he ordered a six-pound lobster. It was priced at $100 a pound at this place. His damn lobster, without sides, cost us $600. By the time we added in his before-dinner drink, sides, wine with dinner, dessert, and after-dinner drinks, the bastard cost us almost $1000. If you have ever seen a six-pound lobster, you would know it would feed a small village. The son-of-a-bitch barely dented it. It wasn't like he was getting it bagged up to take home. He was in

California in a hotel and he lived in New York. I can only hope the kitchen staff attacked the remains of that beast when it came back barely touched.

After dinner Donna slipped back to my hotel room for a night. We were both pretty tired from working the conference all day and we had an early start on the last day of the conference the next day. She had brought clothing for the next day and actually had a room at the hotel, as the conference was being held at the hotel conference center. It made things a little easier for her to be there without raising suspicion. We just had to ensure we didn't enter or exit the same room at the same time.

Donna called me via the hotel room-to-room phone and asked me to come to her room. I willingly did so, only to find her on a conference call. She simply laid back, spread her legs, and indicated she wanted some satisfaction. I got down to business, but she kept talking business as if I wasn't even there. After about thirty minutes, I basically said, "Fuck it" and got up to leave. She stared at me with angry blue eyes as she continued the call. I shrugged my shoulders and turned and left to go back to my room.

About twenty minutes later, I got an angry phone call asking why I left. I explained I wasn't getting her full attention and was tired. She was actually pissed off. She tried to explain how busy she was and that she was able to multi-task. I really felt used at that point. I bid her goodnight and climbed into bed.

The final day on the vendor display, she was in an odd mood. Donna was chatty and friendly to everyone except me. Donna was playful toward the other male sales reps in a way that I had not seen before.

At some point later in the day, as the customers were all in sessions headed up by various industry experts, the vendors remained on the display floor to check our messages and to relax a bit. Our team gathered around our booth and casually chatted about mundane things. The subject of kids came up. All the sales reps had children of various ages. Some were full-grown, some were teenagers, and some were young children like my little Ann. We were talking about parenting techniques. At some point Donna, who had no children, jumped into the conversation and began ripping on my concepts of parenting. I kind of lost it. I told her she had no place in the conversation, and I exited the scene quickly. I got off the hook for a client dinner that evening and enjoyed a solitary meal at the hotel bar.

Around 9:00 that night, I got a call from Donna again asking me to come to her room. I assumed she wanted to apologize. I instead found her nude on the bed, on the phone with a customer. I'd had enough. This time I just turned and walked back out the door.

Shortly after Donna's call, I received a call from my boss advising me to go buy some underwear and fresh shirts. I wasn't going home at the end of the conference. I was headed to San Francisco to work another conference. The endless days on the road and time away from my family were taking their toll.

CHANGE

My life had crashed and was burning. The constant travel was really grinding on me. I hadn't seen my wife or daughter in almost two weeks. I had been travelling constantly for almost seven years now. I had made a small attempt to regain a little sanity by not bowing to Donna's sexual demands. It seemed that I was only servicing her and that it wasn't about me or what I wanted. I'd seen pretty much the entire bag of erotic things she was into. I had participated, as she had wanted. I realized it was about her getting what she wanted and when she wanted it. It never was about me. For single women, having affairs with married men has got to be the ultimate power trip. She uses sex to control the man. He wants nothing more than to have sex. All men want sex and more sex, until you realize all you are being used for is sex, and then it isn't quite so fun anymore.

I had to find a way back to my wife and family. I had to find a way back to the marriage vows I had made and so terribly broken. But whether we would stay together, I knew, would ultimately be Beth's choice. I would have to admit my failings. I would once again have to admit the mistake I'd made. I would not make a fool of her, hiding behind my lie. *She very well may divorce me*, I thought over and over. *She should. I deserve it.* Deep down, though,

I knew I loved my wife. And that I had a sexual problem.

I seemed to have no filter when it came to saying "no" to other women. I didn't know why. It wasn't like I wanted to hurt Beth. It wasn't as if I was angry with her for anything. I just lacked self-control. Unfortunately for me, being honest was going to hurt Beth, and it was going to mean changing jobs. I could not continue to work with Donna. She held my balls in her hand. She could twist and squeeze them for different purposes at her will. If she wanted more sex, she could threaten to go to my boss and tell him about the affair we were having. She could tell him about how I went to Cleveland not to see a potential client who was in town for a Cleveland Browns Monday Night football game, but instead to have sex with her. She could detail several trips I had taken to destinations where she happened to be working with a client and where I happened to not actually sign the prospective client I was supposedly there for. In short, she could get me fired and leave a very ugly stain on my professional reputation.

The only option I could see was to take charge and get in front of everything before Donna could do so. It was going to be ugly, but it was my best shot, and it had to start with my wife. I came home from San Francisco with a plan. I arranged for Ann to spend the night with a friend in the neighborhood. After a pleasant dinner out at a historic restaurant in Saratoga Springs, and a glass of sangria for Beth, I set her down on our couch for the bad news.

"Beth, I need a divorce. I am incapable of being a faithful husband, and you deserve a man who would be true to you."

I felt like scum. I didn't deserve to even be in the same room with her. I told her I had been having an affair over the past year.

Beth said, "Who is it? Do you love her?"

She started to cry. I tried to hug her, but she pushed me

away. There was a look of sadness and anger all at once in her face.

I told her that I'd been involved with a work associate and that no, I didn't love her.

She cried harder and eventually said, "Then why? Why would you screw her? It isn't like I never make love to you. I try to do all I can to make ours a good home. I raise our daughter while you are gone every day, week after week, and this is what I get in return?"

She cried a lot. I cried, too. I cried because I knew how badly I had fucked up and hurt the one woman I really loved.

Beth said, "I have too much invested in our marriage to give up so easy. Hell, I have too much invested in you!"

"What do you mean, invested in me?" I managed.

"You cheated, but you didn't come asking for a divorce because you want to marry the other woman. You came asking for a divorce because you are giving up on yourself."

I replied, "Come on, I am doing you a favor. You know I am a failure as a husband. I am no good for you."

Beth said, "Bullshit! Don't quit on me now if you still love me and your daughter. You're better than that and I know it."

"I may not be better than that. I don't know. You deserve better. What if I am just a failure?"

"Asking for a divorce because I deserve better is worse than just cheating on me!" Beth replied. "Now you get to decide what is best for me, too? Nope. I am not letting you take the easy way out. We are going to fix you, you cheating bastard. I want us to go to counseling, but you have to promise to stop screwing her. I know that deep down you love me. I knew it from the moment you laid eyes on me in room 521 in that hospital. We are going to counseling and getting this fixed. You are going to stop fucking her and we are going to counseling."

I had not considered this option before, but I thought it was the least I owed to her. We'd never been to marriage counseling; no one in my family had ever been to counseling. People in Midwest small towns like the one where I grew up didn't air their emotional laundry out. They quietly tucked it away to grow mildew or got a divorce. That was the way it was in the Midwest. Where I had lived, people scoffed at those "big city" people with their shrinks, or the West Coast hippies with their Zen karma bullshit. No, we didn't do that in the Midwest. But maybe those people on the coasts actually were doing something better for themselves, trying to get help instead of living out miserable lives. I agreed to never see Donna again and to go to counseling.

Beth did some homework and found a marriage counselor who she thought would be a good fit for us. I have to admit; I was still skeptical that counseling was worth anything. Our first session was scheduled late one evening. We sent Ann off again to spend the night with one of her friends from the neighborhood.

We sat down with the counselor, and she began by asking us, "Why do you want to save your marriage?"

Beth answered, "I love my husband and I want our family to stay together."

It was the right thing one could say in this situation.

When the counselor turned to me and asked the same question, I came up with, "I have a problem keeping my dick in my pants and not in other women."

The counselor went back to Beth and asked what she was doing as a mother and as a wife. She spent a lot of time discussing how Beth was not balancing her efforts as a wife with being a mother, that she was devoting much more time to being a mother than to being a wife. She went on to say that if you neglect being a wife, your husband would be vulnerable to the other woman who makes herself available to him. She was coming down on Beth pretty hard. Beth wasn't taking the criticism well. I could see she was getting upset. She was on the edge of tears, and I reached over to hold her hand. She needed someone to be on her side, and I was going to be that person. I had to stand up for my wife. She wasn't guilty of anything except being a great mom and a tolerant wife.

At some point I had to interject. "Hey, I am the one who is fucking another woman! It is me who was cheating on my wife. Beth hasn't done anything wrong."

But the counselor said, "Well, she hadn't been doing too much right, either."

I really took offence to this statement and reminded her again that it was me who was making bad choices; it was me who was traveling to other cities meeting up with another woman.

The counselor then asked me, "Why? Why are you doing the things you are doing?"

I stammered out a bull crap story even I didn't believe that I felt like I wasn't getting enough at home and that screwing around away from home didn't really take anything away from my family. I really didn't know why I was making such bad choices. I'm not sure where she cut me off and started back on Beth again. By the time the hour was up, I felt like I had spent most of my time defending Beth. It then occurred to me that the counselor's plan was by design.

Beth and I came home, and I went to the liquor cabinet and got out a bottle of tequila and two shot glasses. I said, "We need to drink and talk. You need this tonight."

We drank shots of tequila as we reviewed the session. I kept apologizing for how the counselor had attacked her. I kept saying over and over how sorry I was that I screwed up and how I wanted to fix what was wrong. She let loose a lot of anger. I simply pulled my shirt open and accepted all the arrows she could shoot into my chest. I deserved them all.

The next day when we sobered up, we began to realize the full extent of the counselor's scheme. We had fallen into her trap with ease. I was spending all my time and energy defending my wife and explaining what a great person she was. Beth was questioning herself and how she could do more as a spouse, which made me feel even worse. The counselor's tactic had worked brilliantly. We were working together to see the good in each other, not the bad. Yes, I had screwed up big time, but it was clear to me that Beth loved me and wanted to stay married. My thoughts of divorce were the chicken's way out. Beth was right. I wasn't suggesting it to protect her. I was running away from my mistakes again. This time she was not going to let me do it. She was going to force me to "man up" for my family. While I thought I had begun to have feelings for Donna, in the end I realized I was being used. I had been played for a fool and needed to find my way back to where I belonged. I never considered divorcing Beth and not having Ann in my life until Donna suggested it. At this moment the allure of clandestine sex with Donna completely disappeared.

The next step was finding a new job. There was no way I could continue to work for the same firm and have any temptation to fall back into Donna's trap again. I was clearly too weak when it came to her to make good choices. It had to be an absolute termination of the relationship.

I quietly let it be known within my industry that I was looking for a change. Seeking a change is not hard to do when you have a good reputation. A subtle hint dropped to the right person, a whisper to another person, and before too long, headhunters are calling you with opportunities. The right call came in at the right time. Donna had turned on me, letting enough information get to my boss, Bobby, that would make it look like I had been coming on to her inappropriately.

I met with Bobby and said, "Bobby, I've had an affair with Donna from service for the last several months. It was a major mistake. Beth and I have been going through some rough times. We're in counseling now, and I have ended the relationship with Donna."

But Bobby replied, "You aren't the person I thought I hired. I'm not sure if I can save your job, given the allegations."

"Allegations!" I cried, "What allegations? It was totally mutual!"

Donna had beaten me to the punch. I wasn't exactly in a position to fill him in about how I had been used as a sex toy for a woman claiming to be on the straight and narrow AA path, but who was really a sexual deviant fond of snorting cocaine to enhance her sexual pleasures. I reiterated that my wife and I were in marriage counseling and that we'd had a rough patch. It became clear he had no solid evidence of any wrongdoing and felt a strong lecture was sufficient. I let him know that Beth and I were going to take a few days away together as part of our recovery process. Bobby was fine with that idea. The time away was really a trip to Atlanta where I was being recruited as a partner in a mid-sized firm in my industry. My biggest concern would be running into Bobby or two of the other sales reps who lived in the Atlanta area. Still, I knew that Hartsfield was the busiest airport in the United States and I felt the odds of seeing any of the three people I worked with going in and out on a trip there was pretty slim.

I was correct in my assumption. As I arrived at Gate E, I decided to play it safe and walk into the terminal, bypassing the tube. After walking over three quarters of a mile I said screw it to being recognized, and I got on the tube at terminal B and still had a half mile ride left. By the time I met my contacts at the main terminal, I was glad there were no other of my company's employees to be found.

My contacts were both short, pudgy men, one looking to be in his early sixties and the other perhaps in his mid-fifties. Both looked like they needed to spend a lot of time in a gym working with a trainer and a nutritionist. The older fellow was Larry Olsen. He was the principle of the firm at which I was interviewing, Lawrence-Johnson & Company. The other fellow was the number two guy and Olsen's only partner, John Johnson. We departed the airport and drove for what seemed like a long time into what looked like a pine forest. At the end of the road was a new single story office building that housed LJ&C. The firm had about fifty employees. They were a mid-sized regional player in the same industry I worked in and told me they were trying to expand to be a national player. The interview went well and they said an offer would be forthcoming. I flew back to Albany with great hopes it would work out. After seven years of bitter cold winters and being in a really fucked up situation in my current job, this change could not have come at a better time.

The offer did come through, and it came through with a respectable base salary, an aggressive commission package, and a unique twist—an equity position in the firm based on the amount of revenue I generated. The last element really got my attention. I liked the idea of being an owner in the company. Beth liked the idea of leaving New York. She had never wanted to move there and hated the long winters. I accepted the offer and arranged a house-hunting trip.

We selected a real estate agent pretty much by luck. Our agent, Joli, worked hard for us, personally looking at every house we selected in advance of our arrival based on the price range we chose. We saw a lot of houses that were nice, and at the end of the trip the agent took us to a new planned community called Lakeview. It consisted of about ten neighborhoods all with nice up-scale homes, some a little more expensive than others. For our final stop, Joli drove us into a neighborhood named Running Deer. As we drove in, I was blown away by how beautiful the houses were and was convinced we could never afford to live there. She took us to a new-construction house and we fell in love with it, but never thought we could afford it. She ran the numbers and showed us that just with my base salary we could easily afford the house. When I asked about the taxes, Joli said a number that made me laugh out loud. I was so used to New York tax rates that I replied, "Damn, we can never afford the monthly payment!"

"Oh, that is per year, not per month, honey," Joli purred back at me. Southern real estate agents were just so sweet, just like that god-awful sweet tea I learned they serve in Atlanta. I never imagined that we could pay so little. So yes, we could afford the house. We were moving to Woodstock, GA.

I formally accepted the employment offer and set a start date. We put our New York house up for sale and I notified the company of my resignation. I got out before Donna got too much of a chance at extracting any sort of revenge. Anything she said was only to my boss and would be utterly meaningless at this point.

She did come after me full guns, though, when she found out I had resigned. Bobby already knew it was true, but she was adding a lot more in terms of harassment toward me. I had filled him in on enough of the affair to make sure he knew the affair was real, but also consensual. The worst damage it could do would be to cause me not to be rehired there in the future. Donna would most likely end up with a bigger shit stain on her record at the company than I would since I left naming her as the reason I left the company. She would be on the defensive for a long time to come.

Beth was very glad I was getting away from Donna forever. I was hoping that would be the case. It had very much gelled with me how badly I had been played. I felt like a complete ass. I had never had a woman use sex against me while doing it with me. When I was in high school my girlfriend used sex as a tool to get her way. If she wanted to go somewhere I didn't, she would withhold sex if I didn't go along. If I wanted to go to a different restaurant, she used sex to bribe me into going where she wanted. This was a bit different. Donna was having sex with me and using it as a weapon in a different way. Donna knew as long as I was having sex with her, she had something very substantial over me. She could use it with my employer to have me fired and she could contact my wife to ruin my marriage. As long as I was sleeping with her secretly, she held a powerful tool and I was powerless.

I know it sounds absurd, but I know now for sure that Donna selected targets that she used to vent her anger and hatred for her ex-husband. By selecting married men she worked with, she had the ultimate control over her target. Actually, her opening had been to tell me about how she had wanted to be a firefighter. I remembered she'd told me that when visiting a fire station as a skinny fourteen-year-old girl, she had been gang raped by the firemen at the station. When I heard this story after a session of passionate sex in the dark of night with tears in Donna's eyes, I had felt her pain and believed the story. She told it so passionately. She had all the right details. She lived in a suburb of a city near where the fire station was located. She had hung around the department routinely. It wasn't until I terminated our relationship that I began to believe it was just a tool she had used to draw me in, to get my sympathies toward her. She set the hook of a damaged woman who needed my help and love in the form of physical sex. She could lead men down an erotic path until they were in so deep that that had almost no way out. She maintained control by using sex and information about the sex. Donna was a very damaged woman. She had been severely abused in her marriage through alcohol and sexual abuse. There was a part of her I felt sorry for, and I guess that may have come into play as to why I fell into her lure. Maybe it was the same reason I proposed to my wife within a day of meeting her; I knew Beth needed help. She was sick and needed someone to help her. Perhaps this was my Achilles heel toward women; I was attracted to damaged women. I was lucky to escape Donna, but a lot of damage had already been done. My wife would never completely trust me again. That would be a burden I would have to endure.

GEORGIA

There were some wounds still very fresh that would take a long time to heal; in fact, the wounds I had inflicted would never completely heal. The scars would be forever visible in my marriage, and I would have to look at them every day as a reminder of my mistakes. Moving would be an opportunity to reboot our lives.

We got lucky in selling our house in New York. The real estate market at that time was very bad. The state government offices located in Albany, just thirty-four miles from our house, had just laid off several thousand workers after a Republican governor had been elected. General Electric's headquarters, which was only thirty miles away, was being relocated out of state, and a Naval training facility nearby was shutting down. Real estate was not selling quickly, and prices were down.

We found a professor who had recently been hired at a local private women's college to buy our house. We took a large loss on it, but got it sold. Many houses had sat on the market over a year.

I had already driven my BMW to Georgia where I had been living in a temporary apartment. I flew back to help with the last bit of packing. Beth, Ann, and I, along with Buddy, our golden retriever, were driving Beth's Jeep Cherokee to Georgia. We convinced ourselves it would be a fun adventure. But a fun adventure is a day at the beach where you collect seashells and play in the surf. Driving just over 1,000 miles with two adults, a kid entering seventh grade, and a ninety-pound golden retriever is not an adventure. It is more like doing time at Rikers Island. It isn't a long-term holding facility, but you're lucky to get out alive or un-injured.

We did the trip over three days, starting late afternoon the day of departure and only making it to New Jersey that night. The next night was in Virginia, and the third day we arrived in Woodstock, GA. Our possessions in the moving truck were a day or two behind us, so we were staying at the temporary place I had been in for the past month.

Move-in day arrived and went less than smooth. Georgia has red clay. Our new house had lots of off-white carpet. The sod in the yard wasn't completely settled down, and any time the movers stepped off a sidewalk they got red muddy clay on their shoes, which they tracked into the house. They were a New York crew and my complaints were met with a quick "fuck you" or "up your's." At the end of it all the furniture got moved in, we cleaned up the mud, and began the joyful job of unpacking. At least we were in a house we loved.

We were now in a 4,000-square-foot, four-bedroom, three-and-a-half bathroom house with a formal dining room, gourmet kitchen with a breakfast bar and eating area, family room, two-and-a-half-car garage, and a walk-out basement. I was especially excited about this basement because here I could finally make space for my dream of building motorcycles. The curb appeal of our new house was incredible, and we had beautiful, thick, mature woods behind us I could immediately picture walking through with Beth and Ann. There were large, stately old cottonwood and oak trees along smaller dogwoods covering the back third of our property. Cottonwoods have a distinct, very rough bark and can be very tall, some growing as tall as a hundred feet. Ours were probably close to that tall. Our lot sloped downward away from our house so they didn't look as tall until we walked in the woods. It was impressive to think we had such majestic trees on our property. The trees seemed to symbolize strength and stability. Maybe this was the place for new beginnings. Perhaps I could get my head on straight and be the husband and father here that I wanted so much to be.

At least now I could start rebuilding the relationship with my wife in a fantastic home in a nice neighborhood that she also thought was incredible, in warm sunny Georgia. It was a great place for a restart. Beth also felt a fresh desire to attend college. She reminded me she had always wanted to be a teacher. We agreed she should do something about that and go get a degree.

LAWRENCE-JOHNSON & COMPANY

The firm was in deep shit from the day I walked in the door. I had always worked for an insurance company, not an agency also known as a producer. These types of insurance agencies aren't like your run-of-the-mill State Farm or Allstate agencies people are familiar with for their personal insurance needs. These firms work with multiple insurance companies delivering their products to many lenders, sometimes combining products from insurance company A with products from company B and C to build a package that meets the needs of a specific lender's portfolio. For example, a community bank may be buying a lot of auto dealer loans that the auto manufacturer's captive lender isn't taking. These aren't bad risks just not quite the cream of the crop. The same lender may be making residential mortgage loans in the same community, which let's say are in a high-risk flood zone. All of these types of loans require insurance tracking. The auto loan borrowers must maintain comprehensive and collision insurance until the loan is paid off. The mortgage borrower must maintain homeowners' insurance and flood insurance if they are in a high-risk flood zone. LJ&C tracked the status of the insurance of each loan and notified the borrower if they had a deficiency or lapse in coverage. If after a certain period the borrower did not provide the necessary coverage, our firm issued coverage to the lender, protecting their interest in the collateral. The lender passed the cost of the insurance on to the borrower.

When I arrived at LJ&C, they had two major insurance companies who provided insurance back-up for their programs. Within a week of my arrival, I met with representatives from one of the insurance companies. I caught the tail end of a conversation as I was leaving the introduction meeting. I overheard Olsen saying, "He's young and has a pretty good pedigree. We should be able to use that for a while to maintain our needs."

It became clear the only reason Olsen and Johnson offered me an equity position in the firm was because their insurance carriers were concerned about the ongoing livelihood of the business. As both partners were getting up in age, the insurance companies wanted to know about their succession plan. As I had an equity position in the firm, I was being touted as the "succession plan." I would be the guy who carried on the business when they retired, or so they told the insurance company.

They really didn't plan to have me assume any real management of the firm, though. I learned they had pulled this number on a few younger sales people before who quit after a short period of time. This time was different. Instead of an introductory meeting with the firm that was our largest insurance carrier, the meeting went south as the firm cancelled our contract. We suddenly lost almost sixty-five percent of our insurance market. Well, hiring Kevin Owens hadn't been hiring just a pretty face after all. I had connections to big insurance companies that LJ&C had tried to get connected to for years but could not get on their radar.

I made a call to my old boss Bobby who happened to live in Atlanta.

"Bobby, I suppose you know I am at LJ&C now and I need a carrier."

"How much premium are your bringing to the table, Kevin?" he shot back immediately.

"About thirty million." I told him "Are you interested? It is split about 60/40 between auto and mortgage business."

"What happened to your last carrier, Kevin?" Bobby replied. Olsen had screwed them over, and I sensed Bobby knew about that. Word gets around the industry pretty fast.

"Olsen screwed them over." I replied. "Yeah, I know it sounds bad, but the difference is that I am here now, and I am a partner in the business. I am not going to let it happen again." I prattled on.

I set up a meeting and things happened quickly. LJ&C went from being on the verge of collapse to being a producer for one of the premier companies in the industry overnight. Suffice to say my standing at the firm rose like a rocket. Unfortunately, the other proverbial shoe dropped just as quickly.

Our largest client, a bank in Birmingham, Alabama cancelled their contract with us. That contract had made up about sixty percent of our total revenue. We were looking at cutting operations staff for the first time in the company's thirty-year history. Things were pretty stressful. It was also at this point I found out what a litigious bastard Olsen could be when he thought it benefitted him.

First, he sued the lender for wrongfully cancelling their contract. If there was anything I had learned in my ten years in the account management/sales side of the business, it's that you never benefit from suing your clients when they cancel. They cancelled because you screwed up, ignored them, and/or someone else gave them a better deal and was paying attention to them. I guess it is similar to a marriage. Maybe Beth should have "canceled" on me the first time I screwed up, certainly the second time. I guess I was lucky there hadn't been someone paying more attention to her that she could have given her "business" to instead of me. LJ&C had done all three, and a competitor was there to swoop our lender up. Regardless, Olsen tried suing them to make them stay on, and his lawsuit floated like a rock in water.

The lender just said, "Bring it on."

He then threatened suing the insurance carrier writing the business who had just cancelled our contract. Olsen was holding almost $400,000 of premium due to be paid to them. We had a contingent-commission contract, a type of commission that is paid out after the deal closes and the final accounting of the losses on the account are fully realized. Olsen was withholding the final premium payment as leverage to get his contingent commission. He thought he was a smart, tough businessman. In reality, compared to the executives at most of the large insurance agencies, he was a country bumpkin. The insurance companies had lawyers on staff that could keep us tied up in court proceedings far beyond the value of our contingent commission value. I was horrified. This was not how you did business.

I had a passing relationship with the president of the insurance company we were fighting with, and he called me to ask if he and I could meet. I knew I couldn't take the idea to Olsen, so I agreed to do it off the record. We discussed options to get the mess cleared up; that is, for the president of this company to get their premium, he would be able to calculate the final contingent commission and pay it out. The only problem was that no one knew what the final numbers were, as I did not know how much premium Olsen was holding back. That was the key to the final contingent commission calculation. I had to find a way to get the numbers through a back channel.

I was in a pretty good position. I had a deep secret on a person in accounting that had information I wanted. I invited Leslie out to lunch one day, just her and I. I said I just wanted to get to know her a bit better. Once at lunch I told her about the information I needed. She seemed resistant to offer anything up until I said, "I heard a little bit about your freaky side. You've got a little lesbian thing going on behind your husband's back, don't you?"

Surprisingly she did not react shocked or upset. She simply said, "Yeah, I like being with women."

"You're damn bold and brutally honest," I replied.

I was a little worried as she was so casual about her sexual activities that the possibility of me exposing her at work might not be strong enough motivation to give up the information I wanted. I told her again what I needed and why. This time she was quick to agree to give me everything I wanted. She hated old man Olsen. He constantly stared at her and made her feel like a piece of meat. She really hated the guy. Ironically, I had come to believe the old guy was a closet queen as he was in his sixties, had never been married, and, to the best of anyone's knowledge had never dated a woman—or—anyone for that matter. This strategy worked out well. I got the information I needed. All I had had to do was listen to a woman talk about her kinky sex life over lunch one day .

With the newly acquired information, I set up a meeting with the insurance company president. I knew how much money we owed them and he could use that to determine how much money the insurance company would end up owing Olsen. With me knowing all of this, I was in a position to negotiate a settlement between the two companies and further enhancing my position at LJ&C. Of course, Olsen and Johnson could never know that I had gotten my hands on this inside information. It had to appear that I negotiated a settlement in good faith with the insurance company that just happened to be in the range corresponding with the numbers each side was holding. The insurance company was happy to play along, as they wanted to close the books on the LJ&C business.

I went to Olsen and Johnson and told them I had a previous business relationship with the president of the insurance company and that I thought I could get them to pay the contingent commission if they agreed to release the unpaid premium. They needed cash and while they were holding the premium, they could not utilize it. They agreed to let me negotiate a deal. Of course, the deal was already done. I took a quick trip to Birmingham and over a nice barbeque brisket dinner, I sealed the deal. I came back with a $1.2 million check.

It was a really stupid situation, looking back on it now. Olsen was holding $400,000 and thinking somehow that we would have to threaten the insurance company to pay out the contingent commission. All they needed was the final premium to calculate the amount of the contingency, but Olsen was too stubborn to talk to them and give them what they wanted after they cancelled his contract. Olsen had a reputation of thinking he was some brilliant, hard-nose business genius. He wasn't. He happened to stumble into a unique part of the insurance industry at the right time. You could have shown up drunk, fat, and stupid and made money at that time, which he did. For many years his segment of the business was a printing press for money. But some litigation in the late 1990s almost killed the business line. Olsen learned from that time that the best way to get what he wanted was litigation. He had a bad reputation for suing people and companies. It was part of the reason he could not get insurance companies to allow his agency to write their products. I came back from Birmingham a hero. A $1.2 million check would go a long way to prop the company up until I could bring new business in the door.

New sales were challenging. When I joined the firm, LJ&C was a southeastern-based company. Their client base extended as far north as Tennessee and as far west as

Arkansas, but nothing along the East Coast above Georgia; nothing in New England; nothing in the Midwest, Southwest, or far West Coast, either. On the plus side the world was my oyster. I had lots of room to go call on whomever I wanted with the exception of a few accounts that we serviced for other agents. They weren't significant and were not going to take anything away from my target list of prospects.

The biggest challenge I faced was LJ&C's bad reputation. They had sued more than a few previous clients, who had cancelled their business with them. People from those accounts left jobs and went to work at other places. They talked to people, people who were looking for vendors. Word gets around the lending industry about which vendors are better to work with than others.

We also did not have a large number of insurance companies' products at our disposal. That meant when we *did* get to put a proposal on the table, often our competition offered a wider variety of options and pricing. We did have what I could tell was the best insurance tracking technology in the business, though. By then I had worked for some of the major players and the platform we were running was far ahead of anything anyone had at either an agency or an insurance company. At one point, a large auto insurance company where I'd been a systems developer asked to meet with me to discuss buying a version of our software.

The company probably had the third largest insurance IT department in the country. They had an insurance tracking system doing what ours did as well. I asked them why they wanted to buy ours. They said they knew their system was old and dated. It needed major renovations. They feared if they were to rewrite the system in a PC platform, they would simply recreate the same bad system they currently had on a modern technology platform. By buying a version of our system, which they had heard was the best available, they would start with a superior system on a modern technology platform and then modify to meet their specific needs. It would be faster and cheaper and it would ensure they didn't end up with a newer version of the same shitty system they had at that time. Sadly, I could not get Olsen to buy off on the deal. He would only consider leasing the system to them and would not give them access to the source code so they could modify their version of the system. We would have made Olsen millions. The contract could have written a clause into the contract that included language preventing them from reselling or leasing the software. Once again, the old country bumpkin shot himself in the foot.

Sales did start to come in. Some were small, some a little more substantial. I finally hit a gold mine cold calling on a sub-prime auto finance company in southern California. I had a trip to the West Coast and planned to call on three Korean auto manufactures that were introducing their products to the US market. They were still pretty new in America at the time. They were all looking for an insurance plan that would insure the residual value of leased cars at the end of the lease. It was a common product used on American, European, and Japanese cars. Korean cars were new to the American market and the US insurance companies did not have confidence in their long-term value. One company specifically presented me with extensive research data of the quality of their cars. It was over-kill. At the end of the meeting, I told them what they really needed to do was to change the company name to something that didn't sound like a cheap Korean car company. I don't think they found my suggestion funny.

I also set up a call with a sub-prime auto finance firm. They were a pretty big company but not a brand name in the auto finance world as they only worked with distressed borrowers. I met with a team of new players that had been recently hired to grow the company. I proposed a unique new concept that had never been tried in the auto finance industry.

The principals liked it but were not sure about the legality of it. They called in their newly hired general counsel to look over my plan. He came in and listened to my pitch. He then asked the general manager of the firm what they were doing that day. They described their current process of "self-insurance" and how those costs were passed on to their borrowers. He stopped in his tracks and told them to start shredding any paperwork they had on their current program and put mine in place of it as fast as they could. The account quickly became LJ&C's largest account ever. It more than tripled the revenues they'd had from the previous largest client they lost just when I had been coming aboard. I was sitting pretty. I had a lot of leeway in my travel schedule, which prospects I called on and my expenses. I was feeling pretty good. My life in sales was going to finally start bringing in the big dollars I'd worked so long to earn.

After a year, my responsibilities at the firm grew. I gained responsibility for managing the claims department. It had only three people and was managed by about the most honest person I'd ever met, a guy named Craig. He was an absolute Boy Scout, literally was a Boy Scout. He had been one his entire life and was still involved as a troop leader as an adult. Our lenders filed insurance claims with us, and Craig investigated the coverage and arranged payment if the claim was indeed covered.

One of the coverages we provided our lender clients was to pay off the borrower's loan if the borrower stopped making the loan payments and hid the vehicle preventing the lender from repossessing it. A bank in Tennessee filed such a claim on a newer, nice Toyota pick-up truck, and we paid off the loan. Our insurance carrier, of course, ultimately paid the loss; we were just the middle man.

Within a few months, the bank contacted us to let us know that they had recovered the truck. Craig was sent up to Tennessee to get the truck, which was to be sent to auction. The proceeds would be sent back to the insurance company that paid the claim. Instead, Olsen had Craig retitle the truck over to him personally. I was unaware that this ever happened until Craig had been reassigned to report to me. Johnson came across another such truck and wanted Craig to do the same thing titling the truck to him. I told him not to do it, and I went to Olsen and Johnson. They laughed off my concerns, saying they had a contingent commission where, depending upon the loss ratio at the end of the year, the money would come back to them from the insurance company. It was just "advancing" their commission by keeping the trucks. No, it was fraud, flat-out fraud. I was getting a taste of what my partners were really like and I did not like it. This was not what my reputation was in the industry.

Compensation started growing on my end. My base salary quickly became a fraction of what I had been making. My quarterly bonus checks more than equaled the total of what would have been a six-months base salary.

I started enjoying the money a bit. I had always had a passion for motorcycles and stumbled upon an older one being sold by a neighbor. One day, Beth and I were walking Buddy while Ann was at the zoo with a friend and we saw our neighbor Veejay in his garage packing boxes. We asked what he was doing, and he told us he had been transferred by his employer to Boston. I spied in the back corner a motorcycle. It was a Suzuki VX800. It was what was known as a "standard" motorcycle, not a Harley-style cruiser, not a crotch-rocket race style bike or a dual-sport on-off road motorcycle. It was just a regular, beautiful, burgundy-colored motorcycle. I could tell immediately that it was in great shape with almost no miles.

"Veejay, I didn't know you had a motorcycle," I said, trying to sound casual.

"Yeah, I bought it a few years ago and never really rode it much," he said, wiping his brow with the back of his hand. I could smell his wife's curry dish wafting into the garage from the kitchen. "I am thinking about selling it. I can't really ride it that much in Boston."

Beth turned to me and totally shocked me as she said, "Honey, why don't you buy it from him?"

That night I cooked Beth dinner and made passionate love to her doing everything I could to ensure she had an enjoyable orgasm. I bought Veejay's bike and fell deep into the money pit of motorcycling.

The VX800 was not a very popular motorcycle in the US. It was, however, a very popular motorcycle in the UK and Europe. Via the Internet, I connected with a group of guys that had VX800s on the other side of the Atlantic. The headmaster of VX800 knowledge was a guy just outside of London who had four or five of them and probably more spare parts than Suzuki had in their warehouses. His name was Brian. If I needed a part, he either had it or could hook me up with someone in Greece, Australia, or South Africa who had the part. He was a very helpful resource, more so than I could have ever imagined.

Ann was about to turn sixteen, and as I had spent so much of my time traveling on business I told her that I would take her on a trip anywhere she wanted to go, just the two of us, for a week for her birthday. At first, Ann said she wanted to go to Australia, until she realized how much flying there and back would cut into our travel time. So together we decided upon the UK and northern Europe. Her birthday had passed by the time we departed for the trip, but we both agreed it was still a birthday trip.

Word got out to Brian that we were coming over, and he

offered to pick us up at Heathrow airport. We were arriving early in the morning and our hotel in London would not be available until mid-afternoon, so we took him up on his offer.

Brian met us at the airport and drove us to a lovely country cottage in Trottiscliffe, a quaint little village outside of London where he and his family lived. The cottage was more than 200 years old, Brian told us. In the US it would have had a historical marker on the front of it. In the UK it was just a house where people lived. His wife Sarah made us breakfast, complete with clotted cream and scones. We got a tour of the VX800 motorcycle barn where parts were stacked to the rafters. Even Ann was impressed. Brian and Sarah were most proud of their garden. It was a lovely backyard, as we Americans called it. On one side was an old stone wall about five feet tall with English ivy growing upon it. They had a small vegetable garden where different plants were neatly arranged in rows. Their real pride and joy, however, were their strawberries. They were just coming into season and tasted so delicious. They were bright red and plump, without a flaw to them. Afterward, Brian loaned me a motorcycle and Ann and I borrowed helmets. He took us for a tour of local castles, some little-known and a few better-known ones, as well. Brian got us back into London as our hotel became available. With our suitcases in hand and already feeling like we'd done a full day's worth of exploring, we thanked him and agreed to meet him again in five days when we returned from Belgium.

It was a good time. Although the hotel room Ann and I split was small, it had been free with my accumulated hotel points. We explored, seeing all the usual sights. I finally had time to get to know my daughter, and I realized she was a really great person. I couldn't help but feel grateful for the wonderful job my wife had done raising her.

Because I realized that Beth had really done all the work. Goodness knows I had only been a weekend father for so many years. Walking through Hyde Park, Ann pointing to some statue, I began to understand how much time I had wasted chasing the almighty dollar. And for what? My kid was approaching adulthood quickly, and I had missed out on a lot of her life. Sure, we had family vacations flying in first class to enviable destinations, but was that what it was all about? No, my brief appearances weren't really enough in the long run. Being there on a day-to-day basis was what counted, and I had squandered so much of that time.

Well, I had her to myself this week, and I promised myself I was going to do my best to make our trip together memorable and happy. There would be no crazy-ass women pulling off my pants in the hotel room, no drunken bankers dragging me to a strip club, no staggering back drunk to a hotel room in a city that I wouldn't recognize until morning. It would be The Tower of London, Piccadilly Circus, Big Ben, Buckingham Palace, the changing of the guard, the London Eye, shopping, and great food.

We ate at local pubs, where Ann sampled ales alongside her fish and chips, since the drinking age for beer was lower in the UK than back home. We spent hours at Cathedrals were I learned Ann had a keen interest in the knights of old. It was fascinating to see how the knights were entombed directly beneath the cathedral floors, as well as to discover the age of the tombs. We would walk the streets of London during the day and visit clubs at night. We had fun observing the London late-night punk culture. As it turned out, both my daughter and I had a little "wild-child" in us. We laughed and joked about what color we'd dye our hair and how I'd look with a Mohawk. It was a magical few days.

Three days later we took a train out of Victoria Station

through the Chunnel to Midi Station in Brussels, Belgium for our second stop. Another motorcycling friend loaned us a VX800 motorcycle, and my neighbor Richie's sister, who was living in Brussels, let us stay with her.

Ann and I toured around Belgium on the motorcycle for a few days. We ate mussels in Brussels on the Grand Place and had a good laugh about our rhyming skills. Later, we walked around that beautiful square and breathed in the fragrance from all the flowers the flower vendors were selling everywhere. I bought Ann and Beth a box of chocolates from the original Neuhaus Chocolatier. Then we drank beer in the square. I told her that Belgian beers are some of the best in the world. The brewing laws in Belgium state the server must serve the beer in the glass specific to the type. Each brand of beer warrants its own degustation glass. If not done so, the patron is to refuse the beer. They take their beer seriously in Belgium. Enjoying mussels, fine Belgian beer, and chocolate on a warm day in the Grand Place with your daughter is a good day.

We took a train up to Bruges, the lace capital of the world in the Flemish section of Belgium. We had a good laugh as we exited the station. A father in his seventies and a daughter close to my age had exited the train alongside us and asked us something in Flemish. I did not speak Flemish but I recognized it. I also knew that many people from that region spoke French. From the little bit of French I had learned in high school and in my previous travels, I responded "Est-ce que vous parlez francais?" They shook their heads "no". I then asked "Sprichst du Deutsch?" as I understood and spoke a few phrases in German. Again, they shook their head "no." Finally I asked if they spoke English. They smiled and said they lived in Las Vegas. The old man had been raised in Belgium and was bringing his daughter to see where he grew up. We went through three languages to find out we all spoke English!

We were all heading for the old town center of Brugge. We all followed a map Ann and I had and made our way into the old town square saying goodbye and marveling at how small the world can really be at times. Ann was impressed at my limited language skills. I'd scored a "dad" point with my daughter; I felt like a hero.

When our time in Belgium came to an end, we took a catamaran from Ostend, Belgium, which literally translates to "end of land," to the white cliffs of Dover across the English Channel. The catamaran held about forty cars and I have no idea how many people. The trip across the English Channel made me think about World War II and all the crossings the Allied forces had made on the very same route we were taking in the other direction. I could imagine the fear in the young solders minds as they made the bumpy ride across the channel. In their time the boat doors may have opened to gunfire if they hadn't been torpedoed on their way in or bombed upon landing. I knew my grandfather had fought in World War II for the Estonian Army. I don't know, though, if they had been direct allies with the British and traveled this route. He had been taken captive in Estonia by the Nazi, so I doubted he had a Channel crossing. My father-in-law was an intelligent man and became a clerk typist in the US Army. He stayed out of the battlefields as men who could type were worth more than men who could shoot. My dad was one who could shoot. He was in the Korean Conflict. He never did time in the European theater.

The ride across the English Channel gave me chills, similar to those when Beth and I would sit above the USS Arizona at Pearl Harbor. When we arrived in Dover I took a photo of Ann in front of the White Cliffs of Dover, which really are white as snow. I have this photo still; Ann's hair is streaming across her face like some wild horse's mane, her mouth wide open in a joyful laugh.

Brian was waiting for us in his car. The British have such utilitarian cars. Small diesel-powered ones what we would call hatchbacks. They have many of the same manufacturers such as Ford, GM, and Toyota, but the specific models are never seen in the States. People in America like their big, gas-guzzling SUVS. Those are not sold in the UK or the EU.

He took us back to his home where almost fifty people from sixteen different countries around Europe had gathered to throw Ann a sixteenth birthday party. They were all VX800 riders, men and women. Brian loaned us a VX800 motorcycle and we all did a tour around some castles and ruins in southern England. As we stopped at each castle, everyone bought a souvenir for Ann. We stopped at a small but famous motorcycle shop in southern England. The guests outfitted Ann with what the British call a proper kit. That is a complete riding outfit for motorcycling from helmet down to her boots and everything in between. Their generosity was amazing.

I bought myself my first pair of proper motorcycle boots then. They were not the for-show types a lot of Harley Davidson riders in the US wore. These were waterproof with proper-ankle-protection-in-case-you-had-an-accident boots. They were made for people who rode their motorcycles to work every day, like Brian did. We returned to his place to a proper birthday party before calling it an evening back in London. Ann and I returned to the US the next day with memories that we still discuss twenty years later. Ann had the benefit of two sixteenth birthday parties, one at home with her friends and family and now one thrown by complete strangers in a strange land. It made a lasting impression of Europe upon her.

MOTORCYCLES

I t started small: a nice helmet, some good riding gloves, a basic motorcycle jacket. A basic "kit," as my British motorcycling friends would call it. But as it turned out, I had an addictive and thrill-seeker personality. Maybe it explained some of my past fuck-ups with women. The thrill of doing something I knew wasn't really safe, just for the rush.

A friend and neighbor of mine, Richie Casarella, managed a facility that auctioned salvaged vehicles. Some of them were motorcycles that had really very little damage. Sport bikes, also called crotch rockets, have plastic panels on their sides. When they go down in an accident, a lot of time the plastic panels are scratched up and maybe a handlebar is bent, but no serious damage is really done to the motorcycle. Depending upon the value of the bike and how hard the owner pleads with the insurance company, a lot of times the insurance company considers the bike a total loss and sends it to an auction facility like the one my friend managed. A lot of guys—generally middle-age married ones—go out and buy a sport bike they cannot handle. It pisses off their wives, who don't want them riding a motorcycle in the first place. Before they get any miles on the bike, they end up going down in a minor crash and beg their insurance company to total the bike and therefore get them out of it, getting their wives off their backs.

One fine day Richie called me and said he had an almost-new Suzuki GXR600 sport bike that came in with very little damage, scratches, bent shifter and handlebar, and a broken turn signal. GXR600s were pretty hot bikes at the time. He told me he could arrange for the auctioneer to only recognize my bid if I wanted to pick it up. All I needed to do was buy some replacement parts off eBay, turn a few screws and bolts, and have the motorcycle inspected by the Department of Motor Vehicles. If deemed as being fully repaired, I'd have a street-legal, high-dollar sport bike for pennies on the dollar.

I went for it. The day of the auction came and the motorcycle I wanted came up for bid. It was a private auction for licensed dealers only. I got in only through my connection with my buddy Richie.

The auctioneer began the bidding, yelling out, "Do I hear five hundred dollars?"

My paddle went up with several others.

"Do I hear $550?"

Paddles went up.

"Five hundred going once, five hundred going twice, five hundred sold to bidder number seventy-three."

I was bidder number seventy-three. I am pretty sure all the dealers there knew just what had happened, but they couldn't do a damn thing about it.

A little time searching on eBay for the right color body panel didn't take long. I purchased a few minor parts from the local Suzuki motorcycle dealer, but in no time I was ready to have the bike inspected. A local police officer came to my home, a cute woman who knew nothing about motorcycles, and she looked at the bright, shiny, clean bike, browsed over my receipts of purchased parts, and stamped my title as REBUILT. I was to go to the DMV and have a new title issued along with license plates. It was a bit awkward when she asked me to take her for a ride when I got the plates on the bike. I laughed and agreed only if she didn't ticket us for going too fast.

It wasn't long before I sold the old VX800 as I had a nice new Suzuki GSXR600 sitting in my garage. My interest in the sport of motorcycling was growing. I started hanging out at the local Suzuki dealership and bought more riding gear. Before too long, the International Motorcycle Show rolled into town. I made my way down to it and was in heaven. There were so many new toys to check out. There was riding gear, helmets, and new bikes. One caught my eye—a yellow Ducati Monster 900.

Before long I made my way to the local Ducati dealer and traded my GSXR600 for the yellow Ducati Monster 900 I had seen at the motorcycle show. It would begin a long line of motorcycles that would come to almost kill me and eventually save my life. At least my only bad habit now was spending money on motorcycles and gear. No more crazy-ass sexpot women...or so I hoped.

The yellow Monster 900 started my love for powerful bikes. Beth and I were now having routine heated discussions about my expensive motorcycle hobby. The next big bike was a Triumph 955. This one would get me acquainted with the passion for running at racetracks. I didn't participate in professional racing. They were just called "track days." You took your track-prepared motorcycle to a professional racetrack, a grand prix style course where you would run the track for pleasure. Professional motorcycle racing was mainly done on either 600cc or 1000cc motorcycles. I was a novice taking a 955cc motorcycle to the racetrack. I was all balls and no brains. I took the Triumph to a track and was running pretty hot for a long while until in an "S" turn, the back tire lost traction and I started to go down. Somehow, I straightened it back up and got through the turn. When I attempted to shift on the coming straightway, I found my shift lever had been sheared off. I limped into the pit area and called it a day. A rider came in behind me white as a sheet. He could not believe I salvaged the turn and stayed up. It scared him off the track for the day. But I was simply emboldened by my obvious skill.

I acquired an almost brand-new Ducati Super Sport 750 that had been in a minor crash that my Ducati dealer turned me on to. A young guy had bought it and ran from the police when nailed for speeding. He went down in some grass doing very little damage, but he was now in jail and needed bail money. It became my track bike. It was a perfect size for running at the racetrack. Not too powerful so I couldn't handle it, but it still had plenty of juice when I wanted it—and it had the lovely rumble only Italian L-twin Ducati engines can make. My passion for track days was growing.

My motorcycling habit gave me time to reflect. When you are sitting on a motorcycle alone with nothing but your thoughts, it gives you time to reflect. I thought about how I was living my life and what I needed to do to change it. I had a sexual addiction, this I knew. I also knew I was drinking a lot more gin than I should. My one-martini-a-night habit had turned into refreshing my glass two or three times. I was still running away from what I'd done to Beth. She said she had forgiven me, but I hadn't forgiven myself. I wasn't sure if I ever could forgive myself because I didn't know why I had done what I did.

OFFICE LIFE

P art of our sales strategy at LJ&C was to sign up smaller insurance agencies in the same line of business as ours. Their business would be processed on our proprietary computer systems the smaller agents would sell insurance products under our contracts with insurance companies. As smaller agencies, the larger insurance companies we had would not directly do business with them but when their business was aggregated under our contract the business became attractive to them. I had the job of both selling our insurance companies to write our agent clients and to sign up smaller agencies convincing them to put their business under our umbrella. This responsibility was challenging. They knew we serviced some of their competitors. I had to establish a strict protocol to work out who would get a proposal if two agents were calling on the same account.

I had hired a marketing assistant right out of Clemson University who was a savior. Liala helped develop and manage incoming requests for proposals, logging who requested them with a time/date stamp. If the second-in-line wanted a proposal they were informed it was not the most favorable pricing, as that went to number one in line. Unfortunately, Liala quickly became overwhelmed. She needed help.

I went to Olsen and Johnson to get the approval for a

second marketing assistant. I got it without any problem. Having come out of a larger corporate environment, I believed in posting the job internally before going outside for the hire. I got a job description written and posted the job. A bright, young, black woman in operations applied for the position. While she did not have marketing experience, she had several years with the company with great performance evaluations. I made her an offer and she accepted. I had Liala set up a training schedule for her and a cubicle near Liala's workspace that was outside my office. I departed to visit our largest client in California.

During my trip to California, I got an email from Olsen telling me I had to send the new hire back to operations. I was dumbfounded. I called Liala and asked her if there had been any issues in the first few days of training. She reported none and said that everything was going well.

I returned from California and went straight to Olsen's office and closed the door. I asked what the hell was going on. The building was divided by a lobby. Operations, claims, and IT were on the right side. Accounting, marketing, and Olsen's, Johnson's, and my offices were on the left side.

"What the hell is the problem with my new marketing assistant?" I demanded.

Olsen looked me over and slowly replied, "There won't be any *niggers* sitting on this side of the building."

I was dumbfounded. "Larry, what the hell are you talking about? Most of your staff is black! That team out there works their ass off for you and you won't have someone of color sit near you?"

"Kevin you little shit, this is my company and I'll run it any damn way I want. You don't like it, you can pack your things up and get the hell out."

The conversation was over. First off, the use of the "N" word had already been taboo for over twenty-five years and

I was shocked to hear it. It was never used in my household nor was it ever used in my parents' home. To top it off eighty percent of the operations staff including the operations senior manager was black, a woman who had worked for Olsen since the day he started the company.

Olsen was as big a racist as they came. It was fine for black people to work, making him money hand over fist, but they damn sure were not going to sit anywhere near him. I really could not believe what I was hearing.

I told our new hire that I had not thoroughly checked her resume and thought she had actual marketing experience. It was my fault in making an offer prematurely. I ensured she got a pay raise from her previous pay in operations upon her return. She quietly went back to operations. I somehow think she knew what was going on, and I felt terrible. I was even feeling worse about where I was. I had hired in thinking Olsen and Johnson were actually looking for a partner to carry the business on so they could retire at some point. I wasn't so sure anymore. But I did know these were not the kind of people I thought they were when I hired in.

One of the firms I had signed up was out of Buffalo, NY, Simon & Associates. It was a smaller company headed by a guy about my age named Jerry. They had one salesman and a full-time service person named Laura. Simon & Associates was known for providing excellent service. Their reputation was thanks to exceptional efforts by Laura. She was a hard-working woman who went to great lengths to ensure that the company's customers were treated right. As the owner and salesman brought business deals to the table, I worked closely with Laura to get proposals developed. The working relationship quickly turned into a strong friendship. The firm was quickly becoming my fastest growing agent client. The more they brought in, the more money I made. It was a win-win for us to work together.

I started going on implementation calls with Laura. She was an attractive blond with pretty, green eyes who was just a few years younger than myself. I was in Buffalo for a visit with her one trip and had the opportunity to take her and her husband, Joe, out to dinner. He was a minor celebrity in the area, having played professional football for the Baltimore Colts. By the time I met him, he was a high school football coach and teacher. We were out at the Anchor Bar in Buffalo, known for its invention of Buffalo wings, and we were drinking beer, lots of beer. They had a special where you kept the pint mug every time you ordered a certain beer. I'm not sure how many I actually had but I know I left with at least eight mugs.

Laura and her husband had driven in separate cars. She had come straight from the office where she and I had been meeting. Her husband had joined us later. We left at the same time, but Laura said there were a few things she needed to touch base on before I departed. Maybe it was the buzz from the beer, but I didn't pick up on the obvious signals. We went to her car to look over some paperwork. We got in the car and Laura said, "Joe is on cocaine. He has a serious problem and is probably going to get fired. I don't know how much longer I can stay with him."

I started saying how tragic it all was when she leaned over and began kissing me.

"Fuck me now," she breathed into my ear. "Let's do it right here in the parking lot."

This was not the path I wanted to be on, not now, not with her, not with anyone. It was crude, but also a turn-on. She was really attractive, with deep, blue eyes and thick, long, wavy blond hair, but she was also very intoxicated. It wasn't moments before she had her top off. She had very nice breasts, not too large, but sitting nicely on her trim petite frame. I had always been a man who liked breasts and I was trying hard not to do something stupid.

"No, I can't do this. I can't cheat on my wife. You are

really beautiful and Joe doesn't deserve you, but I'm married and I just can't do this," I pleaded.

I was in a tough place. I did not want to alienate her because, if she went back to the principal of the business, she could sway him to move their business. So how do you gently tell a drunken woman that you like her, appreciate her business, but are not going to have sex with her? It was not easy, but I managed to tell her we could discuss our options when we were both sober. It bought me time. Yet I knew I was going to lose the battle. I had a sexual addiction. My sex life at home was fine. I wasn't wanting for anything or being deprived. I just had no control over my desire for the thrill of bedding down another woman. It really was like a drug addiction. I might just as well have been hooked on cocaine like Joe.

I was hoping the drunken evening of proposed sex would be a memory. Laura had been pretty drunk, after all. I was so wrong.

Instead, I began to get more and more intimate emails from Laura to my work email telling me how her husband abused her when he was high on cocaine. She kept proposing meetings that could lead to intimate endings. I kept doing all I could to discourage the thread without being absolutely blunt. Their business line was growing quickly and the revenue grew with it.

Things got awkward when Laura came to Atlanta to tour our office. I met her at the airport, against my better judgment. It was mid-afternoon with the tour not scheduled until the next day. She asked if I could show her my motorcycle collection. I think I had four bikes at that point. I drove to my home feeling pretty safe as my wife was there. I had told my wife where I was going and that Laura would be stopping back to see the bikes. Laura had owned a motorcycle herself.

When Laura arrived at my house, I introduced her to my

wife. Everything was pleasant at first. Next, Laura suggested I give her a ride. I gave my wife a look and she didn't grimace, so I said OK. I gave Laura a helmet and we mounted up on the yellow Ducati Monster. I really thought the drunken sex proposal was well past us and not to be seen again. After a short run up into the north Georgia Mountains to enjoy some tight and twisting roads, we completed the ride and I took her to her hotel. We were to meet later with some of my staff for a business dinner.

I went home and changed into casual business attire for the dinner and went back to the hotel to pick Laura up. I knocked on the hotel room door, which she opened and promptly ran off, saying she would be ready in a moment. I sat in the only chair in the room and waited. She came out of the bathroom wearing a nice blouse and skirt. She sat down on the bed to, I assumed, put on her shoes.

Instead, she leaned back and spread her legs, saying, "I'm not wearing any underwear."

This was a bad situation. I was alone in a hotel room with a woman who had previously proposed sex, now laying in front of me and showing me her nude crotch. How the hell did I manage to be so stupid to get myself into these situations? It was not like I was that damn good-looking. I had done everything not to lead her on, I thought. Instead, I had tried to discourage anything outside of a business relationship.

Laura had now pulled up her skirt and was gently stroking herself, licking her fingers to get them wet. How could any straight man not get turned on? I was losing the battle. She sat up, pushed herself into my face, and said, "Do you want to keep the business?"

So it was blackmail. Screw me or loose the account. I begged her to give her time to think about it.

The business dinner came and went without a problem, and I was able to drop Laura off at the front door of the hotel letting her know my wife was expecting me home.

The tour went well the next day but during the ride back to the airport Laura made it clear she expected more the next time we saw each other. I needed to get away for a while, far away. I called my buddy Richie and threw out a plan to go motorcycle riding in Europe for a few weeks. He liked the idea and we started quickly making plans.

Richie, like me, traveled a lot for business and enjoyed a few cocktails. We booked first-class tickets to Brussels to meet up with a guy I'd gotten to know via my VX800 motorcycle connections. He had a motorcycle rally planned starting July 5 that we were joining in on that would cover a few northern countries in the EU. We would base ourselves out of Brussels and do some day trips and a few overnight ones as well.

Richie and I boarded the Delta flight flying directly to Brussels. We were enjoying a pre-takeoff cocktail as Richie started laughing. When I asked him what the hell was so funny, he showed me his iPhone with the Delta reservations site up showing the cost of a first-class ticket for the flight we were sitting in. It was a few thousand dollars per seat. He laughed again and said, "These assholes are actually paying for their seats and booze! We're getting it all for free!"

I don't know if endless hours traveling on business to earn the airline miles constituted getting it for free, but I liked his thinking. I got another martini as we taxied out to the runway. We had plenty to drink and a good dinner before sleeping most of the eight-hour trip.

Upon landing we were met by a young German guy who was giving us a ride to Antwerp to rent motorcycles. Stejn was a stout, round-faced young guy of maybe twenty-five. He drove us to a motorcycle shop where we had reserved motorcycles. I rented a BMW R1100R and Richie rented a Honda CBR600 sport bike.

Quickly, our situation turned into a comedy of errors. Richie had not gotten his international driver's license. Fortunately, the elderly shop owner was willing to overlook that little item as Richie had a valid motorcycle endorsement on his Georgia driver's license. I attempted to pay the insurance and rental fee on my motorcycle with my American Express card only to learn the shop did not take AMEX. Richie offered to put all four charges—two insurance changes and two motorcycle rentals—on his Visa card. The shop owner ran the first charge and Visa immediately shut Richie's card down for an unrecognized international charge. He had never called his bank in advance to let them know he would be travelling internationally. We attempted calling the toll-free number on the Visa card getting no answer. It was July 4 in the USA. We were screwed. Stejn offered to put all the expenses on his Maestro card, the equivalent of a MasterCard in Europe. We protested and he responded by saying "What is he worst that can happen? You both crash, die, total the bikes, and I have to pay the deductible. Hell, I don't even know you, so it isn't like I've lost friends."

We all had to laugh. The old shopkeeper recalled the AMEX rep had been in recently trying to enroll them as a merchant. He went and found the paperwork, called them and got set up on the spot so he could take my AMEX card. This fiasco was really showing the kindness of the people in the EU. We headed off to our hotel in Brussels, again covered by our points from many nights on the road during business travel.

The next few weeks were good times. Richie and I rode, partied, and rode again. Richie had worked with the US women's ski team back in the early 1980s, travelling around a lot of Europe. He was familiar with many of the places we stopped at, including the best bars. The one firm rule Richie and I had was that if you drank booze, you did not get back on the bike.

We had the hotel in Brussels booked and covered for the entire three weeks we were there. If a daytrip ended up at a pub and the pub had women we ended up talking to, which led to drinks, we would find a place to stay where we were. We both made good money, so the extra expense wasn't an issue. Rich was on track to be in the $300,000-a-year range with bonuses. I was on track to hit a quarter million that year between my base salary and commissions. Pissing money away was not really on our minds. We bought young women drinks even though we were both married. We let them hang on us like we were rich Americans. It wasn't like either of us was going to take one back to the room and have sex with her. We shared the room to keep our costs under control a bit.

We did have one drunken night, though, where a twenty-something German girl came back to the room with us. I hoped Richie was smart enough to have condoms if he scored. I passed out pretty quickly as I was drunk as hell.

The next morning, I asked Richie, "Did you have sex with her?" "Kevin, we both had sex with her at the same time, you idiot," Richie laughed.

I knew Richie. He was full of shit and lying. He probably had passed out as fast as I had.

"Man, don't pull that crap on me. I'm having issues keeping my pants on as it is. I came over here to get away from messing around on Beth. Don't be telling me I was back in the bad-boy saddle," I groaned.

Richie relented, "Shit, I have no idea. I was too drunk to remember anything past getting back to the room."

I suppose we are just lucky she didn't steal our wallets as she was gone by the time I woke up.

During the course of our trip, I jumped onto my online banking site to check my pay deposit from LJ&C. I was due for my quarterly commission as well as my base salary while I was on my riding getaway. Much to my chagrin, no deposit had been made into my account at all, not even my base salary. I had plenty of money in my checking and immediate savings account, so I had no concerns about running short of cash. Still, I was a bit concerned about what was going on back in the States.

Richie and I finished up our tour of northern Europe and returned the motorcycles. Stejn gave us a ride back to the airport and bid us goodbye. As with the incoming flight, Richie and I loaded up on cocktails, the best first-class airline food offered, and slept most of the trip back to Atlanta.

Upon getting back to the office, I saw I had two pressing matters. The first was a request from Simon & Associates to meet with them on a sales call for a large Florida bank. The second was my compensation.

I knew what the first was going to entail, and I had to figure out how to handle it. I made a decision not to have sex with Laura. I damn well knew she was hot and that it would have been really good, but I had made promises to my wife I did not want to break. I had to meet with old man Olsen about my missing compensation anyhow, so I figured I might as well tell him I was being blackmailed for sex. It sounded crazy to me even then, but I thought maybe he would have an answer, something that could help me save the business without cheating on my wife.

I got back to the office Monday and asked Olsen and Johnson to meet. I closed the door and they seemed to know what I was about to say. I think I floored them when I started with the sexual blackmail. I let them know what had gone down short of me giving her oral sex. How Laura had threatened to pull the business if I didn't sleep with her. It was an odd reaction.

Olsen simply said, "You need to do whatever you have to do to keep the fucking business. Understand?"

I was stunned into silence, but then I managed to ask about my compensation. They both shifted around a little, and then Olsen said that I had to agree to sign away my equity position in the firm to continue to get paid. I had not structured the deal to bring me aboard. They had put together a deal that included an equity position in the firm based on how much revenue I generated.

I was beginning to get the picture. I was bringing in too much revenue, or at least too much in that they didn't want to give me the equity that my contract required.

I asked a simple question. "How much am I giving up?"

"We can't tell you that," was the reply.

I told them I was taking the rest of the day to think about everything they had said.

The light was becoming much clearer. My two supposed business partners didn't give a rat's ass if I had to cheat on my wife as long as it saved their revenue. They also were not going to honor the contract they used to pull me away from a much larger company to work there. All I was there for was window dressing to get insurance companies to give them contracts allowing them to write business. They never expected me to generate the amount of revenues I did or to stick around as long as I did. I later found out they had pulled the same scheme on other unsuspecting people like me before.

My first call was to my attorney. I had him draft a letter to Olsen asking for the details of my equity position and letting him know that I would not be releasing it without such knowledge. My next call was to Laura at Simon & Associates. I agreed to meet with them the next day in Ft. Lauderdale to see the prospect. I'd fly down that evening. I knew Laura would be waiting, and I knew where it would end. I was in a really bad place.

When I came home early from the office, I told my wife

everything was fine but that I had to go out of town for a sales call that afternoon. I quickly packed and exited for the airport. I could hardly kiss her goodbye knowing what a worthless husband I really was. She deserved so much better. Beth had never stepped an inch outside of the lines. She would never consider breaking her wedding vows for any amount of money. I was headed off to sell my soul for these assholes who were holding my salary and bonus and threatening my equity position in the firm. I did not deserve her.

The flight landed in Ft. Lauderdale and Laura and Jerry met me at the airport. They had arranged a hotel where we were all staying. Over dinner we reviewed the presentation for the sales call and pricing strategy. It all went well and I was hoping it could be OK. It was one of those hotels where the rooms enter from the outside. All of our rooms were nearby each other. We all went back to the hotel, said goodnight, and went to our respective rooms. I went in and started to relax a bit when I heard the knock at the door.

Of course it was Laura. She was wearing only an oversized T-shirt. She pushed in and it was clear that there was no escaping this time. There would be no taking "no" for an answer. She didn't even ask and I didn't pretend to resist. I simply got undressed and got into bed. She pulled off the T-shirt and climbed in with me. I was screwing to keep my job. I was a corporate prostitute.

Eventually Laura seemed to see my logic from a business perspective for her to leave, and she departed for her room before her boss could see her. I can't say I didn't enjoy the sex, but I also knew she was delusional. Had I led her on somehow? Was it the abuse from her husband that had her looking so hard for a safe harbor? I didn't know. I did know my sex addition once again had taken control of my better judgment. I did know I did not belong being married. I was a failure at the one thing I wanted to be the best at in my life—being a husband.

I arrived back in Atlanta the day after the overnight letter had been delivered from my attorney to Olsen and Johnson. I got to my office to find all of my office packed into a few boxes. I knew what was next. I went across the hall to Olsen's office where he officially fired me. He claimed I had abandoned my job, that my trip to Europe had not been approved. It was bullshit. I took my boxes and headed for home. I called my attorney and asked what would be our next step. He advised me that he would send a second letter advising I had not abandoned my job and that the dismissal was unreasonable. I knew it was pretty much a waste as Georgia was a "right to work" state. It basically prevented mandatory union participation and gave employers the right to fire someone for any reason they wanted. It should have been called a "right to fire" state.

My contract with LJ&C included a non-compete clause. Their attorney had drafted it. I'd signed it when I lived in New York and was eager to move to Atlanta. I had not had it reviewed by an attorney. My primary attorney referred me to a lawyer who was a retired appellate court judge who had gone into semi-retirement. He was well versed in employment contracts. A quick review of my contract surmised it was worthless. It would never hold up in court. It was for too long of a time period, too general in the field of employment I could work in, and a bunch of other things. He agreed to take my case for $3,000. I thought that was a pretty good deal considering this gentleman had his name on one of the largest buildings in Atlanta. In the meantime, I had to figure out what to do with my life. The good news was that I would not have to deal with Laura at Simon & Associates again. I'd given myself up for nothing. My job was gone and I had no care if LJ&C lost the fucking business or not. Frankly, I hoped they would. I wanted to call Jerry, Laura's boss, and tell him what a crazy-ass employee he had and what she had done. I decided, though, it would just make me look bad, so I thought better of it. I had nothing to gain. If he didn't know what had happened, I would maintain his respect. It could be valuable in the future.

The next few days I drank. I drank a lot. I went through a lot of gin. I thought it would help erase what had happened over the past few days. It didn't; it just magnified the mistake in my mind and how I had to hide my mistake forever. Beth saw my pain. Luckily, she saw it as related to the loss of my job. She was wonderful in trying to console me. She had never liked Olsen from the first time she had met him. I am thankful she didn't know the other half of my grief, the disappointment in myself. I was a corporate whore. I was worse than what I had been at my last job, taking the bankers to strip clubs. Now I was the stripper who was actually fucking the bankers.

Depression set in. I'd never experienced depression before. I'd seen commercials on television for medications to treat depression. They were pretty new at the time, and advertising medications was not that common. I knew I wasn't functioning right, but I didn't quite know what was happening. In the meantime, I decided to fuck the corporate world. I wanted to make my mid-life, anti-corporate statement. I did research on traditional Estonian patterns, the birthplace of my mother, and got on my motorcycle. I went out and got a tattoo. I was really showing the world I was my own man.

Ah hell, whom did I think I was kidding? I was a middle-aged unemployed loser with a sex addiction that was certain to destroy my marriage.

I had time on my hands. I couldn't buy an interview with my non-compete contract hanging over my head. Everyone in the industry knew Olsen would sue if they hired me. My attorney was trying to get a court date but Olsen's attorney, Jack Justice, was doing everything he could do to delay a court appearance. I had to laugh at his name. He should have been one of those attorneys who advertised on television with that name: "I'm Jack Justice and my name means you'll get JUSTICE!"

It would have been a perfect ad campaign. The problem was he was a legal hack. Olsen hired him because he was cheap, not good. My attorney looked at my contract and he determined it would never stand up in court. He said it looked like a first-year law student had written it. Olsen was hoping he could get enough delays that I'd run out of money paying my attorney. He had no idea my attorney took the case on a flat fee and was really doing it for fun. I was aware that if I did lose in court, I would be liable for all of Olsen's legal fees. I took a chance.

I thought Leslie in Olsen's accounting department, who was bisexual, might be of some value. I contacted her and asked if she could give me information as to how much they were paying Jack Justice. I felt if I had a running total I would at least be prepared for the worst if I lost. It could have made me take a second mortgage to pay the legal fees, and I would have to find a new line of work as I'd be locked into the non-compete for almost two more years. Somehow, knowing made me feel better. Leslie agreed, with conditions. There are always conditions. She started feeding me information and forming her payback plan. She had a freak side and I knew I wasn't going to get the financial information I wanted for free.

Since I had time, I started going to the motorcycle racetrack more often. I had the Ducati 750 SS nicely set up for the racetrack. It had good, sticky track tires and I had removed all the lights as required for running on the track. My favorite racetrack was a little-known place called Little

Talladega. It was a grand prix style racecourse 1.4 miles long with a nice arrangement of straightaways, S-turns, chicanes, and long, sweeping turns. On the back straightaway I would top 100 miles per hour before coming into a nice long sweeping turn. There was a nice tight S turn that kept your attention, the same turn where I had previously almost dumped my Triumph. It had much more of my respect since that event.

Beth did not approve of my race habit. She felt it was too dangerous. I did my best to tell her it was just a bunch of middle-age guys playing with their toys and no one went too fast.

It was a bit of a financial drain, though. Before losing my job, I had dropped over $1,800 on a full-leather professional racing suit. My race gloves had cost me about $400. My helmet cost $1,000, as did my race boots. Just throwing a leg over my bike, I was pushing $4,500 in gear. I'd picked the motorcycle for under a thousand dollars and only had $800 in replacement parts on it to repair it from when the owner crashed it running from the police. Tires were expensive, but I couldn't remember what they cost. I had banked a lot of prior bonus money and I wasn't telling Beth what I had spent on gear over time. She would have killed me had she known what I'd spent on my hobby.

The track time was a distraction and relaxing. Maybe replacing the danger of hitting "S" turns at high speeds replaced the rush of other women hitting on me.

I caught a break. A software company out of Texas called me and was interested in interviewing me. They were a new company that I had not heard of, but they claimed they had a software system that was better than the LJ&C platform that I had leased to several companies. I consulted with my attorney to see if my non-compete agreement touched on software sales. As LJ&C was not in that business at all when I was hired, my contract did not address it. I had introduced the business line to LJ&C. My attorney felt LJ&C would have no grounds to come after the Texas software company or anyone else hiring me for software sales. I opted to accept the interview.

I met Katharine at the Atlanta airport on a layover she had. The conversation went well. We had a lot in common with business contacts. Her background was in software and I shared my roots in systems development. I had brought a copy of my LJ&C non-compete with me. If this was going to be an issue, I did not want to waste anyone's time. She took her time reading it over and agreed that she saw nothing that would cause her concern should their firm bring me aboard. She asked if she could keep the copy I brought so she could have the company legal counsel review it. I had no problem with her taking it.

We talked about the firm's desire to grow their footprint in the insurance tracking software market. I had an extensive background in the field dating back to my early days as a systems developer and then as head of sales and marketing at LJ&C. I didn't know it at the time, but I had taken several of their clients away as they were operating under a different company name. A smaller Texas software company had been acquired by a large oil company seeking to diversify. They renamed the company and brought in a new management team. I was to be part of the new management team. The interview ended with great promise.

I still had the litigation problem hanging over my head and Leslie was still meeting with me, feeding me financial and strategic information about LJ&C's case. The time to pay the piper came when she said she wanted to sleep with me...while her husband watched. God, where the hell do these freaks come from and how did I manage to find them? She made her case in how she was risking getting fired every time she gave me information.

This time I only thought of Beth and Ann. Hell, I was already unemployed. My life was already in the crapper. Beth had not left me even when I hadn't been making any money. She had stayed by my side. Beth loved me no matter what. It was time for me to start trying to find some sliver of salvation other than in a bottle of gin.

"Leslie, I really need the information," I pleaded to her "If I lose in court you know Olsen is going to come after every dime I have. I need to be prepared."

"You asked me for a favor that can get me fired. You need to pay for the info, honey," she purred. I could hear the smile in her voice.

"You really want to get fucked with an audience, go invite your neighbors over because I am not doing it. I am not cheating on my wife," I yelled, losing my patience.

"Shit, I thought you had it in you! OK, I'll get you the information. Olsen is so stupid he'd never know anyhow."

And so my stream of information about the litigation picked up speed. Once every month we met and she gave me a report of their spending. At least I knew how deep in the hole I was getting if I lost in court. If I lost and had to pay LJ&C's, bill so be it.

That evening, I poured a bourbon, sat down on the back porch, and lit the fireplace. Our screened-in porch with the large stone fireplace was a spot of refuge for me. I had spent many a troubled evening out there, contemplating life while gazing into the fire. Or you could watch the moon move through the ink-black sky. I would watch it all the way across the sky until it began to eclipse the edge of the porch roof. It was best in the middle of the Atlanta winter. It was never too cold in the winter, so you could sit by the fire and stay warm with a drink in the evening.

I liked the cooler temperatures better. My family lineage was Nordic and I didn't like hot temperatures that well. It's odd that I came to live in the south where it is hot a lot of the year. I sat on the porch in front of the fire contemplating what had happened that evening. I was thinking a lot about all the messes I had gotten myself into on the personal side of my life and now on the business side. Losing the job at LJ&C wasn't the first time my job had been pulled out from under me. It happens in the business world to the best of people. I just usually was screwing around with women I shouldn't be screwing around with when it did happen.

I began to see a pattern and an answer. I poured more bourbon, and an answer became clearer. My daughter had already been accepted into Georgia Tech on early admissions. Beth was close to graduating college with her education degree. She would be able to get a job as a teacher easily. I had a Smith & Wesson 9mm in my bedroom and a million dollars in life insurance. It all started to make sense. One accident at the shooting range and Beth and Ann were set for money. It would be quick and painless. All I had to do was make it look like an accident clearing a stuck round in the gun. It would be so much better than her ever finding out what a loser I really was in life.

I had a plan. The question was when and did I have the guts to do it.

Depression is a son-of-a-bitch. It does nasty stuff to you when you least expect it. It dragged me into a hole and convinced me that a bullet to the head was the best thing for my family. I wasn't the classic depression case where you didn't get out of bed for days or fail to maintain personal hygiene. No, I looked and acted what most people saw as normal. Inside, though, I was dying. My mental status was crumbling. I had not heard back from the Texas software firm. I was not getting new information on LJ&C's litigation cost and my attorney was not getting any closer to getting us a court date.

I took a lot of time taking each one of the four different

motorcycles up to the north Georgia mountains riding each week. I was fighting depression, although I didn't know it, and the rides helped boost my spirits for a little while. Beth was in the final stretch of her undergrad studies and spent a lot of time finalizing papers and preparing for finals and the state teacher's test to obtain her teaching license. Ann was finishing her senior year and I was alone at home. Getting on a motorcycle and riding really fast on twisting mountain roads, far faster than I ever should have, felt good. Maybe I was secretly hoping I would miss one of the turns up on Burnt Mountain or on Turner's Pass and be a dead on arrival when the ambulance arrived.

John Lennon has a line in his song "Beautiful Boy" that goes, "Life is what happens to you while you're busy making other plans." I was making plans to end my life, leaving my family with a nice sum of money and unanswered questions they didn't know existed.

Instead, life had another plan. It was rather innocent. It gave me a bladder infection. To be honest I thought that somehow, I had caught a sexually transmitted disease somewhere along the line. It was only for that reason I went to my family doctor. Hell, I could have killed myself with a bladder infection but I damn sure was not going to commit suicide and leave my wife with an STD.

My family doctor was pretty worthless. However, his physician assistant, Peggy, was a gem. She was the only reason we maintained a relationship with the doctor's practice. I made my appointment with Peggy and explained my problem. She took a swab from my penis and had it cultured. As always, she wanted to talk about my life.

"Peggy, I guess my infidelity is an obvious issue. I've made some really bad choices I can't explain even to myself. It isn't like Beth and I are having problems. It is all on me. Now I lost my job. Basically, I was making too much money so they fired me instead of paying me. I've been drinking way too much trying to drown out the pain. In my spare time I go to the racetrack and burn tires off my motorcycle going a hell of a lot faster than I should. It's like I have a death wish or something."

I told her everything except the suicide plan. I didn't realize it, but at some point, I was crying. She stood up and hugged me for a long time.

She said, "I think you are suffering from clinical depression. You have had a lot hit you and you need some help handling it. You need someone to talk to, and I want to put you on an antidepressant medication."

I felt like a ten-thousand-pound weight had been lifted off from me. She said she would check for STDs and get back to me privately on the matter. In the meantime, she gave me the name of a counselor who she felt would help me. I took my prescription and headed to the pharmacy. I was lucky to get a call the next day saying I only had a bladder infection and that an antibiotic had been called in for me. I thanked her and she warned me to keep my pants on. I assured her I would do that.

Who knew a bladder infection would turn my life around? I started taking the antidepressant medication, and within days the sun seemed to shine brighter. My mood improved. Nothing in life had really changed. I still faced litigation. I still had no job, but my outlook was completely different. I was re-engaged in life and wanted to move ahead. What was behind me was over, and there was too much to see in front of me to keep looking back. A call came in from a guy named Glen saying he was with the Texas software company. I asked what happened to Katharine and he said she had been terminated. He was part of the new turn-around team and they wanted to meet with me. This time they would be flying me to Dallas for the meeting. Maybe my luck was indeed changing.

I flew into Dallas and a car drove me up to Plano to an

impressive office complex that was home of the oil company that owned the software company. I met with Glen for about an hour and he had me go meet with some people from the human resources department. When I got there, I inquired as to the nature of the meeting and they seemed a bit perplexed. Apparently, Glen thought I had already been given a formal offer and I was flying in to get all the paperwork for my start date done. I had Glen come back in and we backed the bus up a little. He apologized and said he thought Katharine had made me the offer and that I had accepted. I let him know that that was not the case. He presented me with an attractive base salary of $125,000 a year plus bonuses for the job of head of business development for the software company. I accepted on the spot. The only downside was that I would have a company-furnished apartment in College Station, TX where the software company was located, and I needed to be based there one week out of the month. Well, I wasn't going to be getting a job in my old field with the LJ&C litigation hanging over my head, and the money was good. I could make it work. My wife would have to understand.

The flight home was first-class thanks to my many frequent flier miles. I didn't hammer down cocktails this time, despite my mood to celebrate. I could do that when I got home. I called Beth when I landed with news that I had a job and that we could discuss details when I got home.

She wasn't too happy about the apartment in Texas. We'd done the distance relationship crap when I had travelled extensively, and it had sucked. On the other hand, this was a great base and had the potential for matching the previous money I'd made at LJ&C. At this moment we had nothing coming in and we were living out of our savings account. This was a move in the right direction even if it had a few strings attached.

Lots of good things were happening at home. Beth graduated *summa cum laude* with her bachelor's degree in elementary education. She passed the Praxis, the teaching license test, and landed a job as a kindergarten teacher at a local school. Ann graduated from high school and before we knew it, we were moving her into the dorms at Georgia Tech. She had only looked at and applied to one university and was already headed off to college. Granted, Georgia Tech was only about 35 miles from our home, but she lived on campus. We wanted her to have the full college experience that both Beth and I had missed out on in our youth.

I continued my motorcycle riding as much as I could. It turned out my new boss, Glen, was a motorcyclist as well. He was a unique character. He had worked as a cop, gotten a master's degree in accounting, and then went to work for one of the Big Eight accounting firms. After spending time as corporate auditor, he was recruited to work for the FBI. He was also a killer piano player.

When I was at the College Station apartment, Glen would sometimes come into town and we'd catch dinner at a nice steakhouse. He'd sit down at the piano in the bar and just light the thing up. I had taken piano lessons when I was young but had absolutely no talent. My piano teacher told my parents to quit wasting their money. I really hated Glen for that. He had more talent in his two pinkies for music than I had in my entire body.

Glen, myself, the head of customer service, and the president of the software company, Excit Software, were all new hires starting within a week of each other. The president was a Scottish fellow. Rory Littlewood was his name. He was a damn fine-looking man who was always dressed impeccably. He also had the fucking rich Scottish accent. It was strong enough, but not rough. Women swooned over him. We were the turn-around team the oil company handpicked to get the software company profitable and growing.

I dove in head-first to the new role at the software company. They had a small group of employees from the old firm that had been acquired by the oil company. All of the senior management and most talented software developers had quit when the oil company bought the firm. They were left with an old PC-based system and a newly developed system running on a server platform. They had one large client on the new larger system. The old PC system was the one I had routinely picked clients off from during my days at LJ&C. As I started to learn more about our processing environment, I realized we were in deep shit. The PC platform I knew all about. It was dated and I knew all of its flaws. A rewrite would take at least a year. The larger system was a disaster. A good day was when it only crashed four times. During my programming days, I had worked on systems that didn't crash but once a year. This was beyond bad.

At the same time I was getting a strategy formed at Excit, a client of LJ&C's, Ronald Mantle, called me. He had an insurance agency, which was essentially a competitor to LJ&C, in Virginia that had his business being serviced by LJ&C. I had personally sold him on the idea and had formed an air-tight contract with firewalls between the LJ&C business and his business. There were rules about how prospects would be handled if we both called on them. Once Mantle signed them there were strict rules of how his data was protected in our system so it could not be leaked to anyone for competitive reasons. I went to great lengths to do this. He was the first such insurance agency I signed up and he was a talker. If we failed, he would spread word all over the industry and we would never be able to sub-service another agent. Sub-servicing was very profitable and I made sure LJ&C was not going to screw it up.

Once I was fired, Olsen had other ideas. He would go find a smaller insurance agent near one of the agents he was servicing. He promised them a large account if they agreed to sub-service with him, of course at a higher price than the current agent was paying. Olsen then pulled every bit of data the agent needed to make sales calls to the account and even send LJ&C's internal service people on the calls with them to help seal the deal. The story to the account was most often that their current agent was having financial problems and LJ&C recommended they move their business to the other agent. The transition would be seamless, as the same people would still service it all on the same system.

Ronald Mantle's largest account bought the story hook, line, and sinker. They signed a contract on the spot. LJ&C even had a cancellation letter drafted ready for the lender's letterhead to Mantle. Of course, Ronald got wind of what went down eventually. He hired an attorney and sued LJ&C in federal court for tortious interference. In legal terms it means, "intentional interference with contractual relations, in the common law of torts, occurs when one person intentionally damages someone else's contractual or business relationships with a third party causing economic harm."

I had drafted enough contracts by then to know what LJ&C had done was absolutely illegal. I wasn't surprised. I wasn't there bringing in new business and they had not hired anyone new to take my place. Olsen was getting desperate for new income and he had no bones about screwing other people, even his own clients, to get it. A date was set for my deposition in the case in Atlanta for Mantle's case against LJ&C.

Getting back to Texas for the second week on the job brought a meeting with our largest client. I'd known the players at the company for many years. They were located in Houston. I flew in from Atlanta to meet them for dinner. It was a pretty big insurance company. I met with the president, senior VP of operations, and the senior technology VP. They didn't mince words. Our platform was a mess and was costing them money every day. They had given Excit lots of notice of the problems long before I had arrived and this meeting was simply a courtesy. They handed me a formal letter, giving notice of cancellation of their contract. It was "with cause" as the software did not perform to the standards as required under the contract. Hell, I knew that. The shit didn't stay up and running for more than a few hours at a time. It never should have been released. I wondered how Excit ever got through a demo to sell it. I was convinced it was a series of fudged screen shots strung together to make it look like it was processing in the sales presentation. I let them know I understood where they were coming from. There was no defending the company. We parted on friendly terms with handshakes and them wishing me the best of luck.

When I got into College Station the next day, I called a meeting with Littlewood and Glen.

"Gentlemen, I have some bad news," I told them. "I had dinner with Mark and Andy last night, our largest client. They were not happy with us. In fact, they were furious. Our software is killing their business. They gave me this cancel notice."

I showed them the letter. Littlewood was furious.

"How in the hell did you manage to meet with our largest client and have them cancel our contract in one fookin' meetin', you bugger!" he screamed at me.

He acted as if I had betrayed him somehow.

"Why wasn't I at the meeting?" he demanded. "Rory, I've known these guys for over twenty years and they don't know you at all. You've never even worked in this industry. What the hell did you expect? To walk in here and everyone treats you like some industry kingpin?"

I pushed back too hard. "Listen, our main platform is a piece of shit. It was released to market too soon. None of us were here when it was done so it isn't on us, but we have to deal with it. I am the only one in the room who knows jackshit about this software, and it is crap."

He needed to accept that and address it. Continuing a sales strategy on that platform was a mistake. Given that I was the only one in the room with a software background, specifically in this area, both of them lightened up a little bit. I think they knew I wasn't bullshitting. We did need a plan.

The first plan was to see if we could acquire other software platforms we could market until we either repaired or rebuilt our main product. I would focus my time looking for products and possibly small companies we could acquire, rebadge, and sell until we got our shit together. The next strategy floored me. Rory Littlewood decided that he would force the client that had cancelled to come crawling back to us. He would sue them for improperly cancelling the contract.

I made the mistake of saying, "But they cancelled for cause and I can guarantee you that our software did not perform to standards."

He laid a line of obscenities my way and told Glen to get the corporate attorneys on it immediately. Within two days the former client had a letter delivered from our legal counsel advising them of made-up violations of the cancellation agreement. It wasn't twenty-four hours later that we had a written reply basically saying, "Bring it on— we did nothing wrong."

Littlewood called us back into his office along with our head of client servicing and the head of operations. He asked our head of operations, who had been with the company for a number of years, if she knew certain people who had left the firm when the oil company bought the software company. She did, and Rory asked what they were now doing. She hesitated for a bit but said she heard they had started their own software company. He dismissed her. Rory looked at Glen and asked him about his time at the FBI. He asked if he still had any connections. Glen said that he still knew some people. The next part was surreal.

"Glen, see if you can find anyone to do wiretaps on the phones of the previous employees. We need to verify if indeed our client went over to them."

"Rory, man, I guess it goes without saying this is illegal as hell," Glen said, stated the obvious.

Rory Littlewood laughed and in his thick Scottish accent said, "Get it fookin' done!"

Within the next few days, we were called in and presented with a list of phone numbers. They were calls made from ex-employees who were suspected of forming their own software company and taking away our largest client. We literally called the numbers to see who answered. Most of them were to the client we had lost. It was very clear the group of ex-employees had started a company and indeed taken our client.

Littlewood's evil plan had just begun to hatch. He had Glen do a little more research finding out the legal entity they had formed and had our corporate attorney file a cease-and-desist order to them from doing business with our client claiming they broke their non-compete agreements. I knew most of these people. They were good, honest, by-the-book people. I was in a snake's den. We got back a formal letter from their attorney citing case and point where they had completely complied with their non-compete agreements. This was hitting close to home. I was still fighting a non-compete case myself. I couldn't help feel sorry for them. It was also very clear the client was not going to come back to us no matter how we threatened to sue anyone. *Good for them*, I thought.

I started doing calls on companies with software products that I'd hoped we could rebadge. I was looking for things that serviced some segment of the insurance and lending industry that we were in so we didn't stray too far out of our comfort zone. We also kept up appearances as if we were an active player in our existing space. We attended conferences having a display booth showing our two insurance tracking platforms. It was uncomfortable. Standing on a display floor having potential customers ask you about your products and trying to spin a story was tough when you knew one was as old as dirt and the other wasn't able to run for more than an hour or two without crashing.

Glen was having a difficult time justifying my salary to Rory now that I wasn't actively selling our core computer software. Rory knew why we couldn't sell our existing products, but undoubtedly, he was facing pressure from the parent company now that we lost our largest client.

Glen decided to put a guy under me that would handle implementations and do field service calls. There were no implementations, but we did have a lot of clients on the old PC-based system. We could keep him pretty busy traveling around, doing updates and bug fixes for us.

Glen's wife also worked at the firm. She was the head of operations. Her name was Terry and I should have known she was trouble from day one. She was very attractive. I had learned when she and Jack, my service guy, got married; she was almost sixty pounds heavier. She had gotten her life under control, lost all the weight, and started working out regularly. It worked and she looked really good.

I was in a meeting with Terry and another person on the

staff in my office and I'm not sure how the topic of Sean Connery came up, but I mentioned how he looked a lot better when he was young. She paused, looked right into my eyes, and said, "Oh, I like older men."

I was probably ten years older than Terry. She kept staring into my eyes for what seemed to be a long time. A few days later I was out to dinner with Jack and he had gone to the restroom leaving his phone on the table. It rang and I saw it was Terry calling. I picked it up knowing Jack would be back in a moment. "Hi, Terry. How are you this evening?" I casually answered Jack's phone.

"Who is this? she replied.

"It's Kevin. I'm having dinner with your husband. He went to the men's room and will be back in a moment."

Terry quickly shot back, "You know you are going to be in trouble."

"For answering the phone?" I was puzzled.

She said, "No, I am going to be trouble for you."

Luckily Jack came back and I handed the phone to him. Just what I needed—another Donna in the making.

I returned to Atlanta to do the deposition for Mantle's case against LJ&C, my old employer. I had my attorney come with me and got some of the best advice I ever received: the opposing attorney is there to make you look incompetent. They will use any tactic to make you look stupid, that you are a bumbling fool that should not be believed. It was good advice. LJ&C's attorney immediately went after me for my cause for being terminated by LJ&C. I stayed calm and stated my belief that they simply could not stomach paying the amount that I was earning under my compensation contract.

They poked and prodded nineteen different ways to try to make it look like I was a failure at the firm and deserved to be fired. That would mean my testimony there was vindictive against LJ&C and not truthful. After LJ&C's

attorney had their shot at me, Mantle's attorney had his turn pulling out the details of the contract I had drafted personally with his client, the intent of the contract, and how it was supposed to protect his data from being used in any unauthorized way. I knew the contract well because I had written it. I hadn't gone to law school, but having worked in the insurance industry I had read hundreds of contracts and knew how to write them. Mine were as rock-solid as any attorney could have written.

The deposition lasted almost seven hours with an hour break for lunch. It was a grueling day. I did get a taste of what I would be facing when I eventually got my turn at LJ&C. I'd faced down their attorneys and won. They had not shaken me; they had not flustered me or had any areas of my testimony conflicting.

A few days at home with Beth were much needed. She was now learning how to be a teacher. All the stuff they teach you in college and in student teaching is a bunch of crap. You get hired and thrown into the fire. She was a first-year kindergarten teacher with twenty-four students and, luckily, a teacher's aide.

The reality is teachers learn on the job. There is a huge wash-out rate for first-year teachers. Between forty to fifty percent quit after their first year and go into other professions. I was beginning to understand why the wash-out rate was so high. School systems hire teachers straight out of college, in most cases young women in their early twenties, and throw them into a classroom full of students with no actual idea of how to teach. There really should be a first-year mentoring program where the new teacher shadows an experienced teacher for a full year to learn what the job is before getting their own class. Sure, school systems would pay a year's salary without getting that teacher actually teaching independently, but the cost of not recruiting replacements would more than likely offset the cost over time. I guess that is the businessman in me, looking at the situation. Regardless, it was good to be home and spend time with my wife for a few days before I had to head to Seattle for a conference.

I arrived in Seattle. It was a typical trade show with a vendor display floor where we had a booth. I was a bit lucky this time as Glen said he was sending someone to work the show with me. I checked in and went down to the display floor to begin setting up the booth before the evening activities got underway. I was pleasantly surprised to see Terry already working on the booth. I figured if I had to stand there the next two days and tell lies to people about how great our software was why not stand next to a pretty woman. We finished up the display booth and headed to the elevator. We were at the Westin, which has forty-seven floors. We were both above the fortieth floor, which I was happy about. No street noise if you are above the twenty-fifth floor, I'd learned in my many nights in NYC.

After about floor twenty, Terry and I were alone one the elevator for the rest of the ride up. She gently leaned over to me and whispered in my ear, "I want to fuck you."

It really was all over for me. I had absolutely no resistance on this one. I wasn't going to kid myself any longer. I had no business being married. I had no control over my sexual desires. I think I'd screw a lamppost if it had boobs and asked me to do it. It was just a matter of how long before I filed for divorce. Beth did not deserve being married to a crap weasel. She was a kind and loving woman who deserved a faithful and loving husband. Clearly that was not me. I had no control over what I was doing.

We wrapped up the conference and flew back to Houston. We made the two-hour drive up to College Station where Terry lived. Jack was happy that I was able to give his wife a ride home from the airport. It had saved him from packing their two young kids up in the car for a four-hour round trip.

Everything in life was a mess again. I could not manage to keep my pants on no matter where I was with any woman. I had to ask Beth for a divorce. Looking at myself in the mirror was getting difficult. At least with the money I was making Beth's alimony would be respectable.

At the office in College Station things were tense. The last payment from our now-canceled client had come and gone. We had really no prospects on the table to acquire. I am not sure Littlewood ever went to the board for approval to acquire anything. I was beginning to believe he was "all hat and no cattle," as they said down in Texas. He talked a big game, but he really had no solid business strategy short of suing parties that had not done anything wrong. It was a bullshit strategy and we all knew it. How long was this charade going to last?

I talked to Glen about quitting. I knew things were bad and I said I saw the writing on the wall. He told me to not make any sudden moves and give him a day or two. He came back two days later promoting me from Vice President of Business Development to Executive Vice President and upped my base salary to $150,000 and gave me a bonus check for $50,000. I was shocked. He said he could not afford to lose me and that he had gone over Littlewood's head directly to the board at the parent company with his plea. They signed off.

I called Beth and told her about the base salary but not about the bonus. I had a little something as a reward for myself before I put the balance into savings. I had been eyeing a new Ducati 749R. It was their latest race spec motorcycle that had just come out. It was $24,000. Over the phone I arranged my local dealer to take my Ducati 750

Super Sport as a trade-in. He offered a reasonable price and we cut a deal. We had a track day scheduled for the upcoming Saturday. I told him to prep the new bike for the track and go get my Monster 900 and take that to the track as well. I could break in the new one a little and run the Monster a bit, too.

It was a pretty good day. I had a huge raise, a nice bonus, and, more importantly, the confidence of my boss. He had gone to bat for me big time and sold me directly to the parent company board of directors. That was a Fortune 300 company. This was big time stuff. I had to fly back to Atlanta the next day. I needed to go break in a new Ducati.

I got home and Beth was a very happy camper. A $25,000 raise was substantial. I then told her I had deposited another $25,000 in our savings from a bonus. She really didn't know what to say. Teachers in Georgia with master's degrees and ten years of experience made $50,000 a year. I just upped our income by that amount overnight.

I decide to wait until Friday to tell her about the new motorcycle and the Saturday track day. We went out to a modest dinner at our local Mexican restaurant, enjoying our evening. The mood was festive and light. We returned home and I had high hopes. Going to bed that night was all I hoped for and more. My wife was as passionate as any woman could be. Maybe she missed me; maybe it was the big money coming in. All I know is that making love to my wife was thrilling and I came easily. This was the woman I was supposed to be with. So why the hell couldn't I not screw around with other women? What was wrong with me? What kind of deranged sex addict was I? I wished I had never quit the computer-programming job in Cleveland, Ohio. I wished we had never made that first move to New York and I had started climbing the corporate ladder. Sure, I made big money, but I had lost my soul along the way. There was no way out of the rabbit hole now.

The next day I said, "Beth, I traded the 750 motorcycle for a new one. The dealer gave me a really good trade so it barely dented my bonus. Oh, and…I want—no, need—a divorce. I slept with a woman I work with at the convention."

I could barely look at her. But I continued, "Beth, I have no control over my sexual desires. You deserve a better husband. I'd say I'm sorry, but I know that sounds pretty shallow right now."

She was somewhat in a state of shock. There weren't even any tears this time. It wasn't like she hadn't seen it coming, but she was just vastly disappointed.

She simply said, "Yeah, you've pulled this too many times. I don't know why I can't make you happy, but I don't think it is me. It's you. It has always been you. You have a problem and I can't fix it. So yes, we are finished."

After a moment, I said, "Please go to the racetrack with me tomorrow. Let's try to have a normal day. We could make the divorce amicable for Ann's sake. I will make sure you are both taken care of financially.

"Please come with me tomorrow," I pleaded.

I was a complete asshole. Tell your wife you want a divorce and then say, "Oh, let's go have a nice little outing at the race trace and you can watch me play with my new expensive toy."

She had never been to a track day before. Yet, she agreed to go when she probably wanted to slap me into next week. We drove over to Alabama, where my new motorcycle was prepped and ready for me to break it in on the track. It was a nice June day. The weather was not too hot, so wearing the full-leather race suit wasn't uncomfortable.

I did a few laps on the new 749R and then switched over to my Monster 900 for a few laps. The Monster was like being in bed with a familiar lover. We'd done many laps together and knew how each other reacted to each and every thing. It was a comfortable partnership. I knew where I could push her and where I had to hold back her power. The 749R wasn't as powerful as the Monster 900 but was a race spec bike. Its suspension was set up for race conditions. The engine and throttle response were race-tuned. It was ten years of newer technology than the Monster. It was a wicked beast, but I didn't know it yet.

Between laps Beth and I talked a little. She tried to ask me why, why I kept screwing around.

"Beth, honey," I told her. "I can't even answer that question myself. I don't know. Women make themselves available to me and I just don't seem to be able to say "no." It isn't that I don't love you. I *do* love you, more than you'll ever know. That's why we need to get divorced. If I can't keep my pants on, I don't deserve to be with you. Just know I love you, Beth."

Retreating from further conversation, I remounted the 749R and took off for more laps. I was feeling pretty loose. I was carrying 60 mph into the "S" turn before the long back straightaway. Through the back straightaway I was hitting 120 mph easily before a long sweeping turn. I was getting the bike leaned far over and getting my knee puck planted firmly on the pavement going into the turns.

I officially was taking a training class to qualify for my motorcycle racing license that day. Our local motorcycle shop always had everyone enrolled in some kind of a class on every track day. It was an old insurance trick. If you were running at the track for pleasure and crashed, insurance did not cover your motorcycle. Same thing if you were racing competitively. However, if you were running at the track while in a training class and crashed, your bike was covered by your insurance policy. Being the insurance professional I was, I got my brand-new Ducati 749R covered by my insurance policy before I had ever gotten to the track.

Somewhere in the midafternoon I must had gotten cocky. I must have been carrying too much speed down the backstretch. On the long sweeping turn, I lost traction on the back tire. I must have tried to hang off the bike as they had instructed us in class that day and pushed the bike back upright to recover. It didn't work. The new motorcycle flipped, throwing me directly over it. I landed on the top of my head. Luckily the motorcycle flew over me in the air, crashing into pieces beyond me. The red flag at the pit went up, indicating there was a crash on the track. All the riders knew to immediately go into the pit area.

At some point my wife realized I was not there. The ambulance was headed out onto the track and she had no idea where her husband, the man who had just asked for a divorce, was. It was probably twenty minutes of hell for her before the ambulance came into the pit with me in the back. I was semi-conscious but starting to come around. I had been unconscious for at least fifteen minutes, a medic told me later. It was kind of a comedy of tragic proportions when Beth asked the ambulance drivers about me. They responded that I got hit pretty hard on the head, but I seemed to be coming around. When she asked what she should do, they just shrugged. I should have been immediately transported to an emergency room. I clearly had a massive concussion. Instead, they dumped me with my wife.

My motorcycle buddies helped me out of my race leathers, programmed the GPS back home for Beth, and said they would take care of the rest. She took me home. The next day after calls to my general physician, I went to a neurologist to be examined. The first thing he told us was that I was lucky to be alive. With a concussion as bad as mine, I should have been admitted to the hospital.

During the course of the examination, my cell phone rang. Beth answered it and it was Glen. She had called him earlier to leave a message about the accident and that I would not be in Texas that day.

"Beth, listen, I don't quite know how to break this to you, but the motorcycle accident was the last straw. Kevin is fucking worthless. He hasn't signed on a single customer. Hell, I'm not even sure what he is doing all day but maybe jerking off with his door closed. He's the fucking worst hire I've ever made. He's too high-risk for our company and is fired."

"Glenn, he is being examined by a neurologist right now! It's a miracle he lived through the night and you call me with this bucket of crap. Fuck you!" she cried, and she snapped the phone shut on him. She later told me about all the really terrible shit he had said. But I have no recollection of the event or anything that happened for the next month. People later told me they called to wish me well and that I was incoherent. Sometimes I would call people to tell them something and then call them ten minutes later repeating the same thing.

I don't know why Beth stayed with me. I had just told her I was having an affair; that much I remembered I had told her I wanted a divorce. She should have left me at that racetrack in Alabama to fend for myself. Instead, she had taken me home and cared for me. She took care of me when I didn't know who I was, when I didn't know who she was. She loved me and was damn sure not going to give up on me, again.

We got a break in that my insurance paid the claim on the motorcycle. I got the full price of the motorcycle paid to me less my deductible. I'd totaled the motorcycle with only forty-seven miles on it. That had to be a new record for the insurance company. I also got paid for my race leathers, gloves, and helmet that were all slightly damaged in the crash. Those funds came in handy, as I had no income.

During my recovery, all discussion of a divorce was forgotten. As the recovery went on, I began experiencing frequent migraine headaches. They started off slow after the accident, maybe once every two weeks or so but they began to increase in frequency. I'd start with dizziness. Spots would appear before my eyes and then the nausea would hit. I would have to retreat to the darkened bedroom, pulling a pillow over my head and laying perfectly still in the dark and quiet for hours until it subsided. At my doctor's office, the nurse practitioner prescribed medications to control the migraines, but at some point they progressed to weekly and then to almost daily. She sent me back to see a different neurologist than I had seen after my accident. He put me on a round of medication and we gave it a go for a while—to no avail. The headaches were daily now and getting worse.

My new neurologist finally ordered an MRI. Beth was teaching when I got in to get the results from the MRI. It was a kick in the gut. They had found a tumor in my brain. It was in the area of the brain that controlled pleasure and impulse control. There was no way to know if it was malignant. There was no previous MRI showing the tumor on my brain before. It could have been that size for the past five years, or it could have been half that size a month ago. It looked to me slightly larger than a peanut, but I'm sure it wasn't even that big.

My EEG was normal. The last EEG I'd had done was when I was eleven years old. I'd had a traumatic brain injury as a child and had seizures for a period of my youth. I'd outgrown them, though, and my EEGs from seven to eleven had been normal. My doctors considered me a cured epileptic. They were rare, but in childhood brain injuries can happen.

I now had a tumor in the "pleasure center" of my brain. My first question was how this tumor might have impacted my behavior. My doc said he wasn't completely sure, but that it could have definitely had an impact on my risk-reward reasoning and that it could continue to influence how I made decisions. I asked for his plan, and he said we needed to consult with a neurosurgeon.

I had really been kicked in the gut. I had been through a lot of stuff in my life, but this was something I had never seen coming. I drove home with extreme caution. I got to thinking about all the stupid decisions I'd made and wondered how many may have been caused by the tumor or just because of bad judgment. How was I ever to know which was which? Would I ever know? If it were malignant, would I live long enough to know?

I had to have a difficult conversation with Beth that night. I tried not to drink anything when I got home. I needed a clear head going into this. Adding booze was not the answer, much as I really wanted a drink to calm my nerves. I squashed my temptation to call her at work. Telling her there would do no good and only mess up her workday.

Beth got home and I had her sit down. I produced a copy of the MRI report and the picture I'd taken of it with my phone. We talked about where the tumor was located, how big it was. We talked a lot about the region of the brain and what the tumor may have been doing to me. It was really hard for both of us to digest. It isn't every day someone tells you need your skull opened up and your brain operated on. OK, the neurologist hadn't exactly said that that was what we would do, but he was referring me to a neurosurgeon. To me, that said brain surgery.

Beth was surprisingly calm. Somehow the tumor seemed to make sense to her. My erratic behavior, my dangerous living, the motorcycles, the racetrack, the cheating…maybe it was all because of a brain tumor. Maybe we had hope that a tumor was the problem. Maybe I was afraid it wasn't.

In the middle of all of this my litigation against LJ&C had taken a step in the right direction. My attorney had finally secured a date for deposition. Granted, that was not a hearing date, but it was a step in the right direction. I looked forward to getting in front of LJ&C's cheap-ass attorney again. I had held my own on the first round in the Mantle case. I would kick their asses now that I had skin in the game.

Beth and I began researching neurosurgeons with experience in nucleus accumbens tumors. We found a few scattered around the country but the best guy was in our backyard. He was the head of neurosurgery at Emory University Hospital in Atlanta. My neurologist sent my MRI to him and helped me get an appointment.

The day came, and Beth and I went to see him. He came in and took my MRI films. He left and came back about fifteen minutes later. He looked at me and said, "You're in a pretty bad place right now, aren't you?"

I said I was.

He said, "I'm guessing you exhibit some erratic behavior. You're doing things outside of your usual personality."

I agreed.

He said that not doing surgery wasn't an option and he was open to do the operation on Wednesday. We asked about radiation and chemotherapy. He told us that until we knew what the tumor was, we couldn't begin to discuss those options. They may not be necessary if the tumor was benign.

I don't know if it was the tumor or if I was just being a smart-ass, but I responded, "Ah, so we're talking about this Wednesday or next Wednesday? Because I'll have to check my schedule."

It wasn't like I had a job to worry about, and the fortunate thing was that I was now under the State of Georgia Employees Health Insurance program. I fell under Beth's insurance since I was unemployed. It may have been the best time of my life to be unemployed. The State's health insurance plan was damn good and I was going to need it.

Wednesday morning, we arrived at Emory at 5:30. I was taken back to a special area to prep for neurosurgery. Neurosurgery at Emory is like a different world. The team there is made up of some of the best in the world. Emory is also a teaching hospital. The best doctors in the world come to do their neurosurgeon residencies at Emory.

I was prepped by getting two IV lines started. At the last minute they decided to start an arterial line, an IV that runs directly into an artery. I thought about the time I worked in a hospital as an orderly when I met Beth. I used to hold patients down while we started arterial lines. They are very painful going in. Since I was at a teaching hospital, a resident was assigned to start the line. He stabbed my wrist to the bone five times before a doctor pushed him aside to start the line himself. I understand the need for teaching residents. But sticking someone five times is torture. In less than five minutes I was going to be in the operating room and under anesthesia. Hell, they could have started the damn line then; I would have never known.

Beth looked at me with tears in her eyes and said, "What the hell am I doing here, here with you right now? I should have left you a long time ago. Why are you putting me through this, you bastard?"

I turned to her and sighed deeply. "I don't know Beth. Maybe the dice were loaded against us from the start. Maybe this all wasn't supposed to be; we weren't supposed to be together."

I reached out and touched her hand, and she let me hold it.

"But, maybe we were," I said, smiling a little "Maybe we were supposed to be able to endure the worst that life can throw at us and survive together. God knows how badly I've screwed up and yet, here you are by my side. I didn't leave you and you didn't throw me out. We have survived infidelity, financial ups and downs, good employment, unemployment…we were blessed with a wonderful daughter! And here we are today."

I tried to lighten the mood: "It's only brain surgery. What's the worst that can happen?"

Beth squeezed my hand, frown lines carved heavily into her beautiful face.

"You have to promise me you'll be OK," she said, as the anesthetist came into the room.

"I have some happy juice for you before you go back to surgery," he said. "Give your wife a kiss before you take a nap."

He hooked up a syringe to my IV and began pushing medication. He left and I looked at Beth.

"I love you. No matter what happens in surgery, just know I always loved…." And I was out.

The next eight hours were hell for Beth. They had me on the table quickly and got to work. The tumor was very deep within my brain. It was slow and delicate work. I'm no doctor and I don't play one on television, so I can only imagine how painstaking the surgery must have been. It was about as deep in the brain as it could be and the tumor was removed bit by bit until they believed they had all of it. Take too much and you leave me with irreparable brain damage. Take too little and you may have to go back in again. I have utmost respect for what those guys do. They have egos the size of Texas, but they need it. There cannot be any room for self-doubt when you are messing around in a person's brain.

Emory had a special post-op ICU just for neurosurgery. I woke up there fourteen hours or so after I'd last seen my wife. She looked exhausted.

All was OK until the next morning. I had to piss, but nothing was happening. It was as if they had plugged my pecker with super glue during surgery. I begged with it to piss. I pleaded to pee. I stood up woozy trying to pee, but nothing.

The ICU patient "rooms" were a fishbowl. There was a back area where a family member could sleep, but the front three sides were glass so the nursing staff could see you at all times. There was no privacy. I had inserted catheters as an orderly when I worked at the hospital. I knew the indignity of having someone hold your pecker and shove a tube up it to release the reservoir of piss. I had empathy for every patient I ever had to put one in, and now I was begging them to put one in me. The indignity never felt so good. Prior to doing it, they scan your bladder to see how full it is. I was over ninety percent capacity. In other words, I was legitimately risking a bladder rupture. I ended up with a catheter in me for the next few days. It wasn't a good time, but at least I wasn't exploding. Everything calmed down and surprisingly soon, I was being discharged. I had survived my first brain surgery.

I convalesced at home over the next few weeks, occasionally meeting with my attorney to prepare for my deposition on the case against LJ&C. He was concerned about my ability to handle it so soon after the brain surgery. I assured him if the tumor had not killed me, LJ&C's attorneys wouldn't, either. Ironically, I never heard a peep from anyone at Excit Software. I don't know if Glen or Terry knew I ended up having brain surgery, but people in the industry knew. Word gets around. The people at the small software company in Texas that got sued knew. I had brokered their software to a client in Cleveland, OH before

I had gone into surgery. None of the people at Excit Software ever reached out to me at all. Apparently, all Terry really had wanted from me was a hard cock and now I was out of the picture. I was irrelevant. When I was at Excit Software, I had wanted her like a child wants candy. I now found the thought of her disgusting.

The only contact I got was from Glen. He reached out to me at some point and had arranged a severance package for me. It was $30,000. Given the short time I had been there and all the nasty things Beth told me he said to me over the phone I could not believe he would be offering me anything. He apologized to me for firing me. He said he had caved into pressure directly from Littlewood to terminate me. For some reason Littlewood disliked me from early on. I think it was because the large client had gone through me to cancel instead of him. I really didn't give a rat's ass at the time. I was happy to get the money.

The deposition date for my case against LJ&C to have my non-compete agreement dismissed arrived. I was ready. I came in steeled by the advice I had previously gotten that the opposing attorney is paid to make you look stupid. Well, these bastards were not up to the job. I knew their game and I had my own game ready.

It all started cordially, handshakes and introductions. Everyone except me was wearing nice three-piece suits. I said, *fuck it*. I wore faded jeans, a white cotton button down, and a leather motorcycle jacket. I wasn't playing the corporate game. The initial questions included those about how I came to work at LJ&C, who contacted whom, and whatnot. They asked, as if they didn't know, who drafted my employment agreement. Oddly LJ&C's attorney's asked questions about Mantle's contract with LJ&C. They wanted to know which attorney drafted it. I let them know I wrote it. They asked about my training as an attorney. I cited my years of experience reading and writing similar contracts. They questioned my education and my business experience.

It didn't take long for their attorneys to go on the attack. They first came at me for my supposed job abandonment at LJ&C. I had saved emails approving my vacation time. They came at me for poor performance on the job. I had financial records of the company's growth under my direction. I had an answer for just about everything until they asked about my sexual affair with Leslie from the accounting department. Of course, there was no affair with Leslie. I was concerned they had caught on to her feeding me information about what Olsen was spending on litigation with me.

I took a deep breath and simply answered, "Well, I did find it awkward when Oslen wanted me to watch when he masturbated and ejaculated on her boobs."

It was a total lie, but it had the impact I needed; I got them off-balance. They had no flaming clue what to say. They demanded the response be deleted from the deposition transcript. My attorney asked why they wanted to do that. They had asked a question and I had answered it. They had the transcriptionist stop and exit the room.

I said, "You want to get in the gutter, I'll go right there with you good ol' boys and we can take it all into court with us. Shall I bring up the part about him banning 'niggers' from our side of the building next?"

I hate the "N" word as much as anyone, but I needed the shock value there. These lawyers knew Olsen and had a pretty good idea I was not bluffing. They agreed to wrap up their questions.

We left shortly thereafter. Mind you my attorney was in his mid-seventies and had sat on the bench for at least forty years between criminal and appellate court. We got to the parking lot and he turned to me and told me he hadn't seen any lawyer play a better hand in court than I had in that deposition. After I had completed my undergrad degree, I had seriously considered law school. Maybe I had missed my calling.

Time had come to go back for more brain scans. Had they gotten the entire tumor? Pathology indicated it was not malignant. It was another huge weight taken off our shoulders. At least it was not cancerous.

My dad died of a rare cancer at fifty-three years old that had ended up in his brain. Thinking about my dad had been playing heavily in what was left of my brain.

The scans were run and my neurosurgeon felt he had gotten the entire tumor. He warned me, though, that damage had been done. The increased pressure inside my skull had damaged other parts of my brain, and he told me it would be possible that I might have some long-term issues. He didn't have specific answers at that point, but he wanted me to continue to see the neurologist and monitor my status. The neurosurgeon also said that headaches might be an issue for some time to come due to the severe concussion, trauma from surgery, and presence of a tumor.

The accident at the racetrack hadn't been my first concussion. It had been my fifth. I'd had traumatic brain damage as a child. I'd had two concussions in high school and one just after college in a car accident. A street motorcycle accident had given me a concussion as well. Hell, I was in the same league as NFL players when it came to concussion count but didn't make the same big money.

We'd have to wait and see how things played out. I was most concerned about my behavior. Would removing the tumor change my risk-reward reaction? Would I now be able to make intelligent decisions over immediate pleasure? I really hoped so. Beth stood by me through the motorcycle racetrack accident. Without question she took me home and nursed me back to health only to learn I had a brain tumor. The poor woman sat in an operating room waiting area for over eight hours while I was in surgery not knowing if I would live. The doctors had sat down with us in advance and explained the odds of something going wrong and that I may not live through the surgery. Beth had been through hell and back and had stayed by my side—and for what? If now my brain could be altered and I'd be different.

Mantle's attorney contacted me. He had gotten a trial date against LJ&C in federal court in Washington, D.C. I would officially be served a subpoena to appear and testify. It wasn't like I needed a subpoena. I would have gladly done it. It was a technicality. Since it was a business lawsuit, the expenses were covered under an insurance policy. The policy called for witnesses to be subpoenaed. It's a pretty standard policy most insurance agencies secure and hope to never use. I flew up to D.C. at Mantle's expense, which I found amusing as the man hated to fly. I had met him for joint sales calls almost a thousand miles from his office in Virginia, where I had flown in from Atlanta while he had driven all night to get there.

The hearing, I thought, went well. I got on the stand and was questioned by Mantle's attorney for about two or three hours. He finally turned the witness, me, over to the defense, LJ&C's attorney. He was surprisingly brief. I don't think he had me on the stand for fifteen minutes. I came to understand that there was no way I was ever going to help the defense side of the case. The sooner they got me off the witness stand, the better. It felt good to be a big swinging dick for a day. I'd gotten to stick it to LJ&C royally. Everything I testified to was absolutely true. I hoped the wheels of justice would grind LJ&C to a pulp.

I had to do something for a living. I was looking for options and talking to a lot of my old industry contacts. A Michael Gage, a guy that I'd helped start a firm while I was at LJ&C, needed some marketing support. He felt comfortable contracting me to work with him despite my non-compete with LJ&C. From his perspective I was not under his employ, and he was not a direct competitor to LJ&C as his firm was in northern California. Michael focused on credit unions in northern California and the Pacific Northwest where LJ&C had no business at all.

My regular attorney helped me form a limited liability corporation, an LLC, to put the business under just in case LJ&C tried to come after me. I named the firm Owens.B Consulting, LLC. The "Owens" was for my last name, and the "B" for Beth's first initial. She was my partner in life for now and forever. I thought it sounded catchy, and a graphic artist friend designed a logo for the company. Soon, I was off and running.

The purpose of our partnership was to get Michael's firm into credit unions east of the Rocky Mountains. I had sold products to financial intuitions big and small all over the US, so I thought, *no problem.* I had time, a home office, and I was feeling pretty good. I was only under contract to provide twenty hours a week of my time—so I could really work hard, under promise, and over deliver. Hell, this would be a piece of cake.

I had hard lessons to learn. The credit union market was kind of like a mafia. There were tiers of vendors waiting in line to become the mob boss. Each credit union had their vendor that provided multiple products to them. There was an organization called the CUSO, the Credit Union Service Organization, that was essentially a vendor conglomerate. It had a multitude of insurance products it sold to credit unions. It had them fooled into thinking it was somehow part of the national credit union organization and they had to buy from the CUSO. It was a pretty good act. If the local credit union wasn't buying from the CUSO, it had a line of insurance agents trying to sell to it. They all showed up with donations to their events, contributed to their charitable causes, and did everything possible to be next in line if the current vendor screwed up. Kind of like the mafia when Joey got whacked and Knuckles moves up to take his place in the organization. In this case, as I learned, the vendor second in line waited years before getting the chance to move up to position number one. I thought I could waltz in with a great proposal undercutting price or offering a unique service option and take the business as I'd always done.

I was as wet behind the ears as a newly bathed baby. I worked for six months, taking my partners' money every month without getting squat. I finally got to the point where I had to call him and tell him I had to terminate our contract. I didn't have any chance of cracking the market he wanted in the next five years. He was very understanding and though I lost a client, I secured a friend for life.

Luck was with me, however. My attorney secured a court date against LJ&C on my non-compete case. We were finally getting these bastards into a courtroom. I had faced their lawyers twice now and I was itching for Judge Irwin Stolz, my attorney, to eat their lunch. The court date arrived and we went into the courtroom. Olsen and Johnson were both there. That was a bit of a surprise to me. I assumed they would pawn the duties off to their attorney. I was beginning to believe this was very personal for them now. Their short, fat, little attorney waddled over to our side of the courtroom moments before the judge entered the chambers. He said they wanted to settle.

I was thinking to myself, "You motherfuckers, you drag this out for an entire year just to settle now!"

My attorney calmly told him as the judge entered chambers, "Release my client from the covenants of the non-compete agreement."

Their attorney threw us a curveball, saying they wanted to settle on the equity agreement as well. As part of my employment contract, I got a larger and larger piece of equity in the company as I sold more and more business. It was why they had fired me. They had wanted me to sign away my equity portion without me ever knowing how much it was worth, and I had refused.

Stolz replied, "Well, we aren't suing for that, but we can entertain offers."

At that point he turned to the presiding judge and said, "Your Honor, we may have a settlement. May we have a few minutes in the hall?"

The judge was happy to get a case off her docket. We headed to the hallway. The first thing I told my attorney was that I needed to see the numbers, which he relayed on to the other side. Those bastards owed me just over $800,000. They had asked me to sign away my equity in the company to get my base pay without ever seeing the $800,000 number. No wonder they didn't want me to see the number. They came in with a lowball offer of $50,000. It was denied.

We went back and forth for a while and finally we got to about half of what they owed me when Stolz said, "Kevin, I'd take that offer."

I replied, "Hell, it's half of what they owe me!"

"If we sued and won for the full amount, after court costs and my cut you would not be getting much more," he said.

I looked at him and replied, "I thought you were in for the usual third now."

He laughed and replied "Kevin, I only charged you for the non-compete work. Shucks, I'm disappointed I don't get to argue the case. I had one hell of an opening argument. I would have shredded their contract."

He wasn't taking any more of my money. That man was a saint. We accepted the settlement on a three-year payout. They had to have the first check to me the next day. I had enough income to live for at least four years comfortably. I was also free to work, as I wanted, in whatever industry I chose. I had no non-compete anything hanging over me. I had beaten those sons-of bitches!

I stopped on my way home and bought a nice, new, yellow and black Triumph Speedmaster motorcycle. Yeah, maybe it was a little impulsive, but I was celebrating a long hard-fought battle.

THE NEW LIFE

I was starting over. I had shed baggage from my past with the LJ&C litigation. I had no crazy-ass sex fiend women wanting to bed me down. I was sleeping in my own bed every night with my wife only and loving it.

Did I want more sex than I was getting? Of course, but I had always had a higher sex drive than Beth. The difference now was that I respected my wife's answer of "no" and didn't cave into another woman if she offered it. More importantly, I stopped putting myself in positions where another woman could offer herself to me. I am not bad looking, I decided, but I'm not going to be on the cover of *People* magazine as the Sexiest Man Alive, either. I do think my manner and the way I carry myself had a lot to do with the women I attracted. I also think the corporate positions I was in attracted certain types of women who liked men in power roles.

I now knew that I had a legitimate neurological disorder that was scrambling my ability to make sound decisions when it came to risk, reward, and pleasure. There was a period in my life when I was a normal person in managing this risk. At some point, I began taking on more and more risk for greater rewards. Some of that was drive to succeed in the business world; call it ambition. Somewhere it crossed over into recklessness. The offers, specifically from women wanting to give themselves up to me, blurred. I failed to see the risk associated with the short-term reward. All I saw in the moment was the reward. In these cases, it was an attractive woman promising sexual activity. They were always in spots where they could convince me, or let me convince myself, that I wasn't hurting my wife because she wouldn't know and/or she was miles away. I could not rationally sort out the dangers I was engaging in and the harm I was causing. I now had control over that part of my brain. The monster living in my head skewing my decisions was gone. If I made poor decisions now, moving forward, they were all on me.

I opted to continue my independence as a consultant under Owens.B Consulting, LLC. We had a significant cash flow guaranteed for several years. With what I had in the bank and Beth's income as a teacher, we had Ann's college at Georgia Tech fully funded.

I sold a few of the other motorcycles, dropping down to just the Triumph Speedmaster and a BMW R1150R. The Speedmaster represented the major win over LJ&C. It was a comfortable motorcycle that had good power and classic good looks, but most of all, it represented a victory over the "bad guys." The BMW was a great touring bike. I had hopes of someday taking extended trips with Beth on the BMW. I loved the idea of just her and me escaping the world on the big BMW with her arms wrapped around my waist. No distractions, no work, no cell phones, just us exploring mile after mile of America on a big comfortable motorcycle.

I started working to find consulting clients. It didn't take long. One came to me. It was a large insurance company in Greenville, South Carolina named Liberty Insurance. They had recently been acquired by a large Canadian bank and were projected to be on a big growth path in the US market. I got a call from a guy named Berry, who wanted me to build a suite of insurance products to get them into the banking market. They had no products presently in that space and they saw it as a huge opportunity.

I agreed to meet with them to discuss terms. They were just about two hours from where I lived on the north side of Atlanta. It was a nice distance for a motorcycle ride on a good weather day. I knew their office was business casual, so I set up a meeting. I pulled some mesh riding pants over some dress slacks, put some dress shoes in my saddle bags along with a navy blazer, donned my riding jacket over my white cotton button-down shirt, and headed off to see my new client. As I rode up to Greenville, taking some back roads, I was thinking this was the way to live. Own your own company, set your own meetings, and ride your motorcycle to the meetings. Oh, and best of all, have the client pay you standard travel rates for the whole thing. Hell, I got about 45 miles per gallon easily on the Triumph. I was getting $0.31 per mile in travel expenses. I was making money just traveling on my motorcycle.

We were able to structure a six-month consulting contract without any issues. I had boilerplate contract language ready, and their attorneys didn't have any significant issues with the contract. Berry and I discussed a list of products they wanted to develop. I warned him several of the products had been around for a while and would not be the hottest sellers at banks. He seemed to understand but wanted to have a full suite of products.

I got back on the yellow Speedmaster, returned to Atlanta, and got down to work. Liberty wanted tried-and-true products. It was completely legal and commonly done to simply copy another company's program, tweak it a little, and file it as your own. It sounds like cheating, but it was the normal business practice in the industry. That is exactly what I spent months doing for Liberty. I wasn't a genius. But I did happen to know which companies had the best programs and which ones were not worth borrowing. I took the best and left the rest.

As I was working with the team to get state approvals, I would meet with Berry in Greenville to give updates. I enjoyed the leisurely back-road rides up to Greenville with an occasional overnight stay. There was a great restaurant that specialized in wild game in Greenville not far from the office. I made it a point to arrange an overnight stay once every month just to dine on some elk. The restaurant served a lot of different types of game meat, but none were better than the elk. It made the trips to Liberty a special event.

Two months from the end of the consulting contract, Berry began tossing out comments about me coming aboard to manage the programs I'd developed. I said I was happy as a consultant. But each conversion thereafter, the topic came back up with a little more pressure. In the final week of the consulting term, I went to meet with Berry and he laid out an employment offer: Product Manager with a base salary of $125,000. It was really tempting. I asked him if I would have to move to Greenville, and he assured me that it would not be required. I told him I would think about it. I did a lot thinking on the ride home that afternoon. Beth and I discussed it that night, and we both agreed the steady income would be a good thing.

I called Berry the following day, letting him know that I would accept the Product Manager position. I also told him, as we did not currently have any clients, that I would agree for a short period to do sales work to get the product line off the ground, but I would not continue to do sales more than a few months. I was not going down the hellhole of constant travel again. I knew the damage it could do, and I had already done my time on the road. He agreed and thought it was generous of me to be willing to take on sales for a period. I was back in the corporate world again, much to my chagrin.

On my next trip up to Greenville, I was officially given a nice office. I didn't bring anything but two family pictures to put in the office. It wasn't like I would be spending a lot of time there. I would maintain my home office in Atlanta and travel up to Greenville every other week for two days. In the mean time I started prospecting potential clients. We had a broad suite of products, much wider than I'd had at LJ&C. Liberty was more interested in products that were related to life insurance and credit insurance. After all, they were at heart a life insurance company.

I decided to start focusing on the New England region as banks in that area had a better reputation of using life and credit insurance products. My strategy was to hammer away at one region first and not bounce all around the country. It would allow me to go to the region, make a series of sales calls over a few days, and get back home. New England was more compact. It wasn't as spread out as, say, California or Texas, where you could call on one prospect and then drive half a day to see the second. In New England, you could call on three banks in Boston by 1:00 pm and see a fourth in Providence, Rhode Island by 3:00 pm, without breaking a sweat.

I worked banks in Connecticut, Massachusetts, Rhode Island, New Hampshire, southern Maine, and Vermont. New York was impossible to get our programs approved, as you had to have a life insurance company domiciled in New York to do life and credit programs there. We felt there wasn't enough business to warrant the expense at that time. I started making inroads to several banks. One specific bank was a bank in Rhode Island. No company had ever sold them a credit or life insurance program before. I made a good contact and it was looking like I may make history there.

The staff at Liberty was great. They were a very welcoming group. One of the women who worked closely with me, Darlene, who filed my programs with the state insurance departments, raised and showed Newfoundland dogs. My golden retriever Buddy was getting very old. She and I talked a lot about me possibly getting a puppy from her when the time was right. It was nice having a normal office relationship with a woman. She wasn't flirting with me. There was no sexual tension. Maybe I was doing something different. Maybe I was just around better people. I didn't know, but everything just felt normal at the Liberty offices. Darlene had an assistant that was drop-dead gorgeous, and I really didn't care. She was just a member of the team. I didn't lust after her. She did her job well. She came to my office and asked questions and left with answers. It was just like how normal offices are supposed to operate.

Working mostly from home when I wasn't traveling helped. Beth and I were getting along much better. Clearly my brain surgery had changed me. I think I was better, but I did have times where my personality would be off. I couldn't put my finger on it, but I was just a little spacey at times. Overall life was pretty good.

It got a whole lot better one day when I got two phone calls, as I was about to depart for Greenville. A bank in Boston and the Rhone Island bank, the elusive holy grail of insurance sales, both agreed to purchase insurance programs from Liberty. I was ecstatic! I got my gear packed up and threw my leg over the Triumph Speedmaster for the ride up to Greenville. I got to the office around 11:00 am and headed straight for Berry's office.

I sat down and said, "Berry, you're never going to believe this! I got a call from both the Boston bank and the Rhone Island bank this morning. They have both agreed to contracts! This is incredible. No one has ever sold insurance to that account in Rhode Island. We literally made history in our industry, buddy!"

I was glowing.

Berry didn't look excited. In fact, he looked sad.

"Kevin," he said, rubbing his face, "I got a call from our

159

managers in Canada this morning. They are pulling our operations budget for the product line."

I looked confused. "How are we going to service the new accounts?"

I still didn't get it as he turned to pull a file out of his desk drawer. He turned to me and started apologizing. I still didn't quite understand what was happening until he actually said the words: "Your position is being eliminated."

I sat there, stunned. I had been employed just less than six months. Berry said something about doing all he could to take care of me and that I would get a generous severance package. He felt terrible after how hard he pushed me to come aboard. I was in shock. He said he would get the details of my package to me within a day. I got up and headed for my motorcycle.

On my way out of Greenville I stopped at a Kentucky Fried Chicken to get some lunch. A tiny old woman was in front of me, having ordered the least expensive meal on the menu. She was counting pennies out of her purse.

I stopped her and said, "I'll pay for your lunch."

I had no job; I had no idea what my severance package was going to look like or where my next dollar was going to come from, but something told me that buying that little old woman's lunch was the best thing to do that day.

Afterward, I took the long way home through the north Georgia Mountains. I felt calm riding the Triumph home that afternoon. I somehow knew after all I had been through that I would survive this as well. The weather was delicious and I had a relaxing ride. The sweet Triumph treated me like a therapist that afternoon, easing my concerns about life.

I arrived home and gave Beth the news. We still had two more years of the structured settlement from LJ&C coming in, so it wasn't like we were going to be hurting. She felt bad that I'd given up my independent consultant business only to have the corporate position blow up so quickly due to no fault of my own.

The next day a FedEx package arrived from Liberty. It contained the details of my termination and severance package. I am not sure how Berry did it, but he had indeed taken care of me. I was given a six-month's salary. In addition, he calculated the commission I would have potentially earned on the two accounts I landed and somehow got Liberty to pay that as well. I had a check for the equivalent of one and a half times my annual salary in my hand. I could not believe my eyes. I did not hesitate for a second to take it to the bank and immediately deposit it. I didn't want some executive in Canada suddenly changing his mind on my package. I thought back to that little old lady at the Kentucky Fried Chicken in Greenville. I learned something about random acts of kindness that day that has stayed with me ever since.

Lady luck continued to shine on me. As I was looking for consulting clients when I signed up Liberty, I had also called on a local company in Atlanta. It was a large international insurance concern but they didn't have any lines of business to which they felt I could add value.

Two days after my severance package from Liberty arrived, I got a phone call from a gentleman named Dave Mulligan. He worked for the Atlanta firm I'd called on as a consultant. He wanted to know if I was interested in working as a consultant with them. I said I'd be happy to meet to discuss his project. He was out of California but would be in Atlanta within the next week. We set up a meeting.

The firm, Affirmation, was looking to get in to auto insurance tracking and lender-placed insurance coverage. They were already the dominant player in the equivalent mortgage business. They tracked insurance for some of the largest mortgage servicing companies in the country. They believed that those companies, which also had related auto lending business, would gladly sign Affirmation up to do their auto insurance tracking and lender-placed coverage. My job would be to design insurance policies for them.

Dave and I met and worked out an agreement. Like my contract with Liberty, I would have a six-month contract to get policies developed. They had an extensive compliance team that would work with me on getting the state approvals done. The money was good and we moved forward.

It didn't take but two months before Dave threw out the offer to come aboard as the product manager for his new product line. This time I didn't hesitate. This was a very large local company. I had actually worked for a part of the company many years before when I lived in New York. The Miami-based company I'd worked for had merged with an Atlanta company to form Affirmation. They had grown to become a large international Fortune 300 company. It was a place where I could blend into the background and just be an employee. If this product line didn't work out, they had lots of other jobs that were much easier to get to if you were already on the inside. I accepted the salary offer that matched what I'd recently had at Liberty plus a generous bonus plan. Most importantly, I would not have to travel. No sales at all. We had two sales people in place for the product line.

I showed up for my first day in the Atlanta office and literally no one had any idea who I was or where I was supposed to go. I was escorted up to the seventh floor of the eight-story building and parked myself in a cubicle. A little after noon, someone finally came by and said they had talked to Dave in the California office about me. He had failed to notify the local human resources department that I was starting that day. I was moved to a window office. Which was nice, except I had no idea what a product manager at Affirmation actually did for the company. I got through the first day and went home to my wife. I was perplexed. I had a well-paying job, but I just had no clue what I was supposed to be doing.

We had a person who worked remotely in Clemson, South Carolina who had been with the company for twenty-seven years. She had originally worked for the Miami company when the merger happened. She moved to Clemson when her husband retired. She had come down to Atlanta to meet with me at a dinner the same day Dave came in from California. The two sales people came in from their remote locations for the dinner as well. It was my first team meeting on the job.

I arrived at the restaurant and met Janet, a woman of about sixty. I suspect she had been very attractive in her younger years. She'd gained some weight but still had wonderful blue eyes and a pleasant smile. She clearly had consumed a few cocktails and gushed a little too much over me. I really was a bit uncomfortable with a woman just about my mother's age clearly flirting with me, but luckily the rest of the team arrived and we got down to social business. The next day Janet apologized for her behavior. She said she had had way too much to drink and had acted like a fool. I told her it was OK, and all was forgotten.

The team went to the Duluth, Georgia processing center to meet the newly hired guy who would head up our operations department. We had picked him up from a large auto lender that had exited the business. He was a great find. He was smart and personable. I could never manage operations staff. I had no tolerance for the bullshit that went on in the day-to-day petty politics in the call centers and data entry worlds. But Jimmy, as he preferred to be called, had a sweet spot for all of it in addition to understanding budgeting and computer systems flow.

One of our demonstrations at the Duluth office was the pride and joy of the Affirmation company, their FlowSmart system. It was a system that "read" incoming insurance documents using pre-built templates looking for key words. It had been designed for the mortgage operations. There were nowhere nearly as many mortgage insurance companies as auto insurance companies and therefore not as many formats in the business for the declarations page, the document that the borrower was required to provide as proof of insurance to their lender. Affirmation thought they were the smartest people in the world with their system. Sometimes when you are a large company, you get so big you forget there are walls and don't look beyond them. They truly believed no one in the industry had anything better than what they had for processing insurance documents.

I looked at it and grimaced. LJ&C's system blew this system away. The LJ&C system was using Optical Character Recognition (OCR) that could be trained to dynamically read insurance terminology and grab data off a document from anywhere no matter how the document was configured. The FlowSmart system could only batch similar policies together and look in specific places for specific data. If the data was not clear, it was kicked out as an exception for human review. The systems I'd leased to companies a fraction the size of Affirmation had systems that were light years ahead of these guys, and they couldn't believe me when I told them that.

The division president had joined us for a meeting at the operations center. We got into a discussion and he started bragging about how great the FlowSmart system was and how we were going to toast the competition in the auto space with it. I should have known better, but my mouth got ahead of my brain. I began to tell him the system was actually antiquated compared to all of our competitors; even small insurance agencies were running better technology. He was furious. I tried to explain that I leased the LJ&C system that had OCR and I also had brokered software for a firm out of Texas using even better technology. Template-based software had not been used in the auto insurance space in years. In addition, most of the insurance information was being fed directly to the insurance tracking companies via electronic transmission in a standardized format, completely by-passing hard documents at all. It was called EDI, or Electronic Data Interface. When our team would be making sales calls on potential auto lenders to track their insurance, the questions would not be about how fast we process paper documents. The questions would be about what percent of our incoming data was EDI. His FlowSmart system, his pride and joy, was a dinosaur in my business line, and I'd just made him feel like a dinosaur as well. He left the meeting pissed off.

I survived the first week by the skin of my teeth. The division president's office was next door to Dave's from California, and they were not only work friends but close social friends as well. Their families vacationed together frequently, went out to dinner, and had neighborhood parties. Dave was able to calm him down, explaining my background was exactly why he hired me. They needed someone from the outside, someone who knew what was going on in the industry. I at least now knew what job I had to do. I had to build an EDI interface as well as revamp the FlowSmart system to use OCR instead of the template-based processing the company had used for the past fifteen years. It was an aggressive plan, and it wouldn't happen overnight. I wasn't so much of a product manager as a I was a *project* manager. Our two sales people were out beating the bushes for customers. I was hoping they got some—but not too fast, as we were nowhere ready to start processing them.

I decided to start on the EDI side. We could get EDI from about sixty percent of the major auto insurance companies in the US. The data came in in a standard format. Our cost would be low, and if we hit a big lender, we could limit our data entry hiring to manage the physical paper until we got the OCR part of the system built. I already had contacts in the EDI world and it didn't take long to secure all the contracts I needed. As a bonus the mortgage side of the business jumped on the bandwagon and decided that the crazy EDI idea sounded pretty good. The mortgage side of the business suddenly reduced their data entry cost by fifty percent. I may not have been popular with the division president for making him look like a dinosaur, but he damn sure liked what I was doing for his bottom line.

One of our sales guys, Walter Frombach, finally made a sale. Actually, it was the best kind of sale possible at the time. It was a product to an auto lender that collected premium on every loan made, but we didn't track the borrower's auto insurance. It was a fairly large lender and started producing around $80,000 a month immediately. We finally had a little revenue coming in. Our five-year plan had us up in the fifty-million-dollar annual range by the end of year five. I had no idea where Dave ever got that number.

Our other sales person, Brooke, had been calling on some very large prospects. She finally got one to agree to come into Atlanta for a tour of our operations center. It was somewhat of a sham. We were tracking one small bank on the East Coast that we'd somehow stolen away from an insurance agent that was an existing customer. We'd bring a bunch of extra people from the mortgage side of the business over to the auto processing side for the tour and tell them to bring up processing screens and occasionally pick up the phone and pretend to be talking to an inbound caller. It was all show and no-go.

The tour came and went just fine. Our actors played their parts well. No one knew the difference if they were on real calls or not. We had them directed to one processor that had a pre-set screen up and showing what we wanted them to see. As they walked by the rest, the screens looked similar but there was no way they'd know if what they were seeing was auto or mortgage info or gobbledygook. Our scam worked and Brooke signed them to a "tracking-only" deal with promises their insurance business would soon follow. The account had over 100,000 loans, so it was a major boost to our operations area. Still, it was not a real revenue stream. The price we charged for tracking was not even break-even. We would be making our money off the insurance product when we got it. Little we knew it would never happen. They had played Brooke.

Walter and Brooke, as I had done in my sales day, worked conferences. We were trying to get word out on the street that Affirmation was a player in the auto insurance tracking-and-lender-placed insurance business. One of our biggest competitors was my old California employer. They had a fifty-million-dollar block of insurance agent business that we were chipping away at. I started to occasionally go to a conference to try to meet with agents and get them to move their business from them to us. I was a logical choice as I had signed a number of their accounts.

At a conference is Las Vegas; about six years since I'd last seen her, whom should I happen to run into but my old lover Donna. She'd had a significant boob job and still looked pretty good. She had aged a little, but the years had been fairly kind to her. She was a redhead now. I wondered if she was still matching the carpet with the curtains. We exchanged pleasantries, talked shop for a few minutes, and went our separate ways. Nothing about our affair ever came up. It was as if it had never happened.

I really wanted to run after her and ask her, "Why me? Why did you choose to fuck me?" I wanted to slap her in the face. I wanted to inflict the kind of pain and shock Beth had felt when I told her I was having an affair with Donna. But somehow, I knew slapping Donna wasn't the answer. It was a sick, stupid thought. She probably would have enjoyed it as she had been into S&M. I was embarrassed at myself for even thinking such thoughts.

Some questions would never be answered. Maybe I didn't really need to know the answers. Jimmy Buffett's song "Margaritaville" popped up in my thoughts as I walked back to my hotel room, alone: *"...and some people claim that there is a woman to blame, and I know it's my own damn fault."*

Perhaps the affair with Donna had been my own damn fault. I couldn't continue to put the blame on her. I had to own it and accept responsibility for my mistake, all of my mistakes.

I would never see her again and that was just fine with me. My perverted idea of revenge would never be.

Our one salesman, Walter, was struggling through a divorce. He'd been married about thirty years and I don't know if it had started to fall apart before or after, but he'd met a woman at a conference that worked for a large bank. They ended up attending similar conferences over about a year, and when Walter's divorce became final, they officially became a couple. He moved from Ohio to her home in Florida. Dave, our boss, was furious. Dave was a practicing Catholic and the divorce didn't sit well with him. The idea that Walter immediately moved in with a woman he'd met at a work conference really bothered him. I believe as punishment he moved him out of sales and under me to do whatever I could find for him to do.

I saw a great opportunity for him managing and growing the agency sales channel. He grabbed that bull by the horns and was off. Meanwhile, I'd sold a new product I developed to a sub-prime auto finance company that Brooke didn't want to call on. Walter was killing the agent market, increasing its revenues monthly. My team was responsible for ninety percent of the revenue the division was generating. My review and bonus plan were looking pretty good.

My life was finally running smoothly. I was making good money as a base salary and thanks to the work I'd done on computer systems development that benefited both the auto and mortgage tracking businesses, I scored a pretty impressive bonus after six months. It was in the range of $50,000, so I decided to buy Beth an upgraded wedding ring set with a substantial diamond this time. She was very pleased.

Next, I gave myself a little reward. I had pretty much all of the money from my severance package from Liberty still in the bank and I had another two years of the structured settlement from LJ&C due. There was a BMW motorcycle dealer about three miles from my office and I decided to take a ride over one day at lunch. They had a new model that had just come in—a F650GS. It was actually an 800cc motorcycle, but they named it after a famous dual-sport that had won the famous Paris-Dakar rally several years before, the F650GS. It had gone out of production and this was a reintroduction of the model. They had a red one in stock and, well, I had to have it. I traded my older BMW 1150R and got a good value for it. I added a set of BMW hard locking saddlebags and a GIVI top case. I loved a GIVI top case. It was a perfect place to store a full-face helmet when you got off the bike. I also got the key to match my saddlebags. I was in heaven. It was my first new motorcycle since the unfortunate day at the racetrack. This was not a crazy go-fast bike. This was a dual-sport motorcycle that I'd set up to use commuting the twenty-seven--mile route to the office. I liked my car at the moment, a BMW Z3 convertible, but spending time on a motorcycle every day would be a great way to clear my head after a day in the office. No, Beth wasn't thrilled, but she didn't protest too much since I'd gotten a good bonus and decent trade for the other motorcycle. She really was much too kind.

Ann, on the other hand, and for the first time in her life, wasn't ranked number one in her class. She was pulling excellent grades, but the people sitting to her right and to her left in class had all been ranked number one in their high school classes as well. Georgia Tech had been a very difficult school to get into, and, as we learned come the second year, even tougher to stay in.

During her freshman year at lunch one day, which was at an English pub that reminded us of our week in Europe, I asked Ann, "Why Georgia Tech? MIT was sending you letters; there were lots of universities you could have gotten into. Why pick one almost in our backyard, kiddo?"

Ann paused over her fish and chips before answering, "Dad, Georgia Tech is one of the toughest and best engineering schools in the country. And you know what else? They have a pretty decent football team."

"A good football team? How in the world did that drive your decision?" I was perplexed.

She's five feet tall and, well, a female.

"Materials Science is a tough program. Not everyone makes it through to the end. I am going to be stressed to the max at times. I need an outlet. I am going to be in the marching band and do color guard next year."

She had participated in marching band and color guard in high school. She figured a university with a good football program would have a good marching band. She was right. Despite having no college of music and the marching band being under the school of architecture, it was a good band.

She tried out and made the color guard squad. It was one of her best college decisions. First off, it gave mom and dad a reason to buy season tickets to Georgia Tech home football games. Neither Beth nor I ever lived on campus or had the traditional American college life, so we made up for it when our daughter was in college. I traded my BMW Z3 for a yellow Jeep Wrangler with a black top matching Georgia Tech's school colors. We bought a premium parking pass each season and became expert tailgaters. We got the fold-up GT chairs, a fold-up table, a portable grill, utensils, a cooler, and everything else we needed to do a proper college tailgate.

We'd cook up all kinds of great food before the game depending on the game's start time. I loved to cook, especially grill, and Ann had always loved my grilling when I got home from a week on the road when she was little. Beth and I would arrive by 10:00, mix Bloody Marys, and I'd make breakfast sandwiches of egg, bacon, and cheese on a grill with toasted English muffins. A later start meant burgers or brats with all the trimmings. Ann would always join us for tailgating, usually with a few band friends. We were known for having damn good tailgate food and drinks. After tailgating, there was a tradition of where the band met to play at a fountain and then they marched down a street to the stadium.

Those were some of the best memories of my life. During that time, Beth and I reconnected as husband and wife and as proud parents. Being in the marching band also meant Ann went to the college football bowl game every year she was there. She had trips all over the country each year for bowl games, as luckily the team was pretty good during her entire college career. Ann was acing college.

Life at Affirmation was going well. Beth was well established at her elementary school, getting great reviews as a teacher. It was amazing to see how gifted Beth was at teaching. For years I had known she was intelligent and had boundless patience. After all, she had stayed with me when anyone else would have kicked me to the curb, and rightfully so. But Beth had a special degree of patience and caring that only a handful of teachers possess. Dealing with kindergarteners all day is unique from all other grades in teaching. On the first day in all other grades, students have an idea of how to be a student. But in kindergarten some of the kids had been to a preschool, whereas some had never been more than a few feet from their parents' side. The same was true for parents. For some parents it was their first child to enter school and it was terrifying to send them into the unknown world. Some reacted better than others. Beth had to steer the boat through all these sometimes-troubled waters and produce capable little first graders at the end of the year. She had the sad job of identifying children that had significant learning disabilities and fight not only to get the school system to provide them extra help, but to get the parents to recognize the situation and accept it.

It was at this point in my life, now that I was not traveling every day of the workweek, for months and years on end, when I began to fully appreciate how wonderful of a woman my wife had become. We married so young and my blind ambition had taken over my life. I fought to climb the corporate ladder and really ignored my family in doing so. My tumor, I believe, had influenced so many horrible decisions that should have ended my marriage. At this point I was now finally able to objectively look at a more mature, confident Beth with new eyes. I now wished I had seen this all along. I had been so blind and now so much damage had been done.

A friend told me once that when it comes to your dog, if you do it right, you get countless days of joy and one incredible day of sadness. The sad moment came as our beloved golden retriever, Buddy, who twelve years before had ridden down from New York in the back of the Jeep

Cherokee, was at the end of his life. He had been the type of dog everyone loved. People who didn't like dogs loved Buddy. Buddy came from a jumbo line of golden retrievers out of the New England area. His lineage was all one hundred-pound dogs, though he wasn't fat at all. He was just a very large dog. We were amazed we had him as long as we did.

As December came around in Ann's first year of college, it became clear that Buddy was no longer doing so well. We took him to the vet and she confirmed he was beginning to shut down. A week later, we had Ann come up from school to join us at the vet. We circled around our beloved dog that had been with us romping in the snows of New York, that had gone leaf-peeping with us in Vermont as a puppy, the dog we'd snuck into a B&B in Maine, and that had become the friend of everyone in our neighborhood in Georgia. We all cried. The vet administered the first dose of medication to relax Buddy, and he fell asleep in my lap. The second dose was administered, and his heart quietly stopped. He gently came to the end of his life. Our sweet, gentle giant was no longer with us. We'd never again try to calm his fears in a thunderstorm or take him for an ice cream cone in the back of the Jeep. I felt like a part of me died with him that day.

As we left the vet's office, our tears stopped. Buddy had made the passing easy for us. He knew his time had come to pass long before we were ready to let him go. As we left, we knew he was out of pain and had lived a good, long life. I don't know if I will ever have as good of a dog as Buddy again.

That night I went to bed for the first time in a very long time without my beloved dog at the foot of my bed. My house felt empty and, despite Beth being there, I felt slightly alone. I lay in bed and pulled Beth close to me. I thought about the suicide plan I'd once considered to hide from the mistakes I'd made, and the pain I would have caused her if I'd gone through with it. I thought about how she might feel had I done it. Would the house feel empty and alone to her if I had chosen to kill myself? Or, would she have been happy to have a way out of the marriage? It wasn't a subject I would ever be brave enough to discuss with her.

Two months after Buddy's passing, Beth and I were watching the Westminster dog show that is on television in November. The Norfolk Terrier won the show and we both thought they were pretty cool-looking dogs. He'd had golden retrievers for the past twenty-two years. We discussed getting a smaller breed. I told Beth I'd do some homework. The Norfolk sounded great until I found out there were no breeders in our area and the closest one, over five hundred miles away, had a litter of pups coming up in about a month. I was told a thousand dollars would be fine for a deposit on one of them. The total cost would be closer to three thousand. Beth and I agreed we would not be getting a Norfolk Terrier no matter how cute they were. We started looking at breeds that looked similar to Norfolk Terriers and saw Cairn Terriers were similar and a lot less expensive. We found a breeder that had a litter available right away for more like $500. We went to the breeder and Beth picked up the first puppy that came to her. I think the little fella knew no woman was going to say "no" after holding a cute little puppy in her arms. We got a Cairn terrier puppy we named Nugget.

THE CRUMBLING CORPORATE WORLD

Things at work were going well, so I thought. I was working with the IT team, building a new service for the sales team to sell the skills of our claims department. As that system came online, I got notice from my boss that I'd been selected to join a group of other employees from the company in Aspen, Colorado for an event called Top Team. Each year the company would reward the top-performing employees in the company with an all-expenses paid, weeklong trip to a nice location. The year before it had been Hawaii. Beth would be coming with me, and I was thrilled for us to be together in such a beautiful place as Aspen.

We were flown out first-class and put up at the St. Regis Hotel, one of the best hotels in Colorado. We took in the sights, enjoying great meals and great company-arranged activities such as mountain horseback riding and hot-air balloon rides. The summer weather was perfect—warm summer days with bright blue skies and cool, comfortable nights.

One of my favorite experiences was a walk we took to the John Denver Memorial just outside of downtown. It was a quiet spot by a babbling mountain stream in a grove of aspen trees. There was a large boulder with lyrics from his song, "Rocky Mountain High" carved into it. You could really feel his spirit there.

There was a book in our hotel room about aspen trees. As Beth was enjoying a leisurely bath, I read that Colorado aspen trees are the world's largest living organisms on earth. The root system of the aspens is all interconnected, all part of the same tree, if you will. Interesting little facts you learn when you have time to relax and study nature without the pressures of the world on your back. I suppose it isn't too different how people are all interconnected in some way. For some odd reason I thought back to Donna and how she seemed disconnected from the world. I momentarily felt great sadness for her and what she seemed to lack in her life when we were together.

Maybe it was the high attitude air, maybe it was the thrill of being treated like celebrities by the company, but Beth and I had some of the best sex since our honeymoon on that trip in Aspen. She was playful and innovative. Maybe I had just needed to give her a reason to want to feel sexy. I was so thankful she had not divorced me.

At the end of the week the group of employees gathered for a final dinner at the top of a mountain at a ski lodge. It was awards night.

Team after team was called up and given accolades for their performance for the company during the past year. As the names kept getting called out, the evening was getting late and my team had not been mentioned. I assumed since our department was new that we would not be seeing any special recognition. The fact that we were invited to the event was enough for me.

Then it happened. The company president called my name and then the names of the members of my team. We went up on the stage, and first, each of my team was given awards for their efforts in building the department. He finally turned to me, the man who had infuriated him when he was a division president, who was now the president of the international company. He called me over, shook my hand, and announced to the crowd that I was promoted to director and was head of The Business Unit of the Year. I was shocked.

I looked over at Beth, who was beaming at me. I had received the top honor for the entire corporation as well as a promotion on the spot. He handed me a beautiful hand-blown glass trophy, which he kindly said they would ship back to the office for me. It weighed at least ten pounds. It came with a nice bonus check as well.

I made my way back to my seat and could tell for the first time in a long time my wife was truly proud of her husband. It felt good. I hadn't screwed anything up. I had under-promised and over-delivered. Though I felt that I still had a long way to go with Beth, I showed up every day for this company. I did my job very well; important people had recognized it. Now the entire international corporation knew it as well.

The next day was a blur as I received congratulations from people on the streets of Aspen. I assumed they were Affirmation employees who had seen me get the award. I felt like a celebrity in a town known as a celebrity hangout. For a few minutes, at least, it felt good to be king.

Back at the office, Walter was still killing the agent market, having increased our revenues over $30 million a year. I think he was actually glad to be out of sales and under me. He was doing great getting agents to move business to us. He had a lot of contacts in the industry and they were paying off for him.

Janet had been moved under me as well. Since I'd been promoted up from the Product Manager position and she was nearing retirement, I opted to promote her to Product Manager, my previous position. She was more than capable. It also gave her a $30,000-a-year salary increase. She had been underpaid almost her entire career at the company. The least I could do was make her last few years a little more worthwhile and boost her Social Security earnings numbers when she did retire.

I felt bad for Brooke. She was working hard in sales but getting no breaks. She had not closed a premium-producing sale in the four years I had been there. She had a lot of talent and a ton of contacts, but nothing was happening for her.

In the meantime, Dave was awarded control of another department. I can only assume it was because he was the company president's buddy because it sure wasn't because of talent. He was a very analytical guy who was now asking me to spend my day producing all kinds of crazy spreadsheets on our business showing nothing. It was busy work and I pushed back on it. I instead starting working with a data analytics group in Atlanta to glean all the information Dave wanted out of our computer systems and report it to him routinely. But I had miscalculated. I thought Dave and I were pretty close. He had confided in me that the director of his newly acquired department was not someone he felt could do the job. He asked if I could manage both departments. I didn't want to throw anyone under a bus, but the other director wasn't the brightest bulb in the lot, and I told him, yes, I could do a better job managing both departments.

In a few days I got a call to meet Dave in a meeting room. I walked in to find him sitting there with a person from HR. Like my last meeting with Barry at Liberty, I didn't get it at first.

I joking said, "Oh man, you never want to walk into a meeting with your boss and find someone from HR sitting there."

He simply said, "Yeah, it isn't good for you" and began to walk out.

I'd been terminated. My job eliminated. "Dave, are you kidding me?" I yelled, as he turned back to face me. "I am responsible for ninety percent of the revenue for the department. I don't know what your other director is making for the company, but I'll bet she hasn't brought in the change like I have in my short time here."

It was fruitless. He turned again and walked out without saying another word. He went with the other director to manage both departments together. She had twenty-eight years with the company, only two years from retirement. Hell, I only had four years. I would have made the same decision based on that aspect alone. I wouldn't have been able to terminate someone two years from retirement. Had he been a man and discussed it with me, though, I would have gone to Janet and offered her a package to retire. I would have happily gone back to being Product Manager. I had never wanted to manage staff or multiple departments when I had hired in. I wanted to come in, do my job, and quietly hang around until I could retire.

The HR person escorted me back to my office, where a box was waiting. She watched me pack my personal effects, including my blown-glass trophy I'd recently received for being named as the director of The Business Unit of The Year. That was a ten-pound paperweight now. *What the fuck?*, I thought looking at the HR woman. Did the company think I was going to go to the supply cabinet and steal $10,000 worth of pens?

I got my few personal things together and reached behind the door for my motorcycle-riding suit. When she saw it, she asked if I'd ridden my motorcycle that day. It seemed kind of obvious that I had, as most people don't wear a one-piece motorcycle suit to work unless they rode a motorcycle that day. I laughed out loud. Pretty much everyone in the home office knew I rode a motorcycle to work. Many said I would get killed on the crazy Atlanta expressways. I had joked back, asking, "How bad could you get hurt getting hit at three miles per hour?" The HR rep frowned at my box and said she would have a service deliver the box to my house for me. She escorted me back to the first floor and, at the front door, relieved of my company ID card.

I went out, got on my motorcycle, and rode to the nearest gas station. I called Janet and Walter to fill them in on what had just gone down. They could not believe what had happened. I asked Janet to contact several people I had meetings scheduled with that afternoon, particularly in IT who had been working on the data-mining project. Janet and Walter told me to stay in touch like all people do when this shit happens. Most of them never mean it. Walter did. Beth and I were invited to his wedding shortly thereafter in Jacksonville, Florida. I visited Janet once at the amazing home her retired husband built by himself in South Carolina, but the relationship quickly faded.

STARTING OVER, AGAIN

Time once again to start over. This was getting old, and a recession was starting to hit the country. The letters "V" and "P" behind my job titles on my resume would prove to be a curse shortly. The recession of 2007 came to be known as the "mancession." Forty-something-year-old, six-figure guys like me got creamed. If you had been at a certain level or above, you could not buy an interview for anything.

I had many a conversation where I heard, "You're overqualified and made too much money in your last job. You wouldn't be satisfied here."

My reply was always, "My income today is zero and my mortgage company still wants to be paid. How about we talk?"

Click.

Beth had been handling the termination fairly well. We'd been down this path more than a few times. She was there with me only a few months before to see me get the highest honors in the company's awards banquet. She knew I hadn't screwed anything up. But it was time to resurrect Owens.B Consulting, LLC. Hell, if I couldn't find a job, I'd go make myself one.

I talked Beth into us attending my thirtieth high school reunion. She had never attended any of hers and was not particularly a fan of them. I, on the other hand, had been on the planning committee for my fifth and tenth reunions before we moved to New York.

At the reunion, I ran into an old friend who had become a world expert in rocket engine technology. I jokingly said to him, "Too bad you don't hire materials science engineers. My daughter is looking for an internship."

She wasn't. She was planning to work at the college bookstore over the summer and just pretty much relax. He said they hired them all the time and to send her resume. In two weeks, our daughter was on a plane to southern California to spend the summer as a paid intern at the company that made all of the rocket engines for the US space program. It would be a great start to our daughter's engineering career.

Life wasn't doing too badly except my headaches were coming more and more frequently. I was seeing a new neurologist, who had tried a variety of medications including Botox injections around my skull, which was an experimental treatment for migraines. Nothing was working. She finally decided to send me for a spinal tap to measure my inner cranial pressure. It was a long shot, but nothing else so far had worked. Maybe I had inner cranial hypertension.

She was right. My pressure measured going into my spine was off-the-charts high. I was sent home from the hospital with instructions about what to do post spinal tap. One of the things I was to watch for was a headache, which I though was ironic as I had headaches every day. Well, as I found out, they were nothing compared to what happens when you have a leak in your spinal cord.

Over the next few days, I was incapacitated due to headache pain. I finally broke down and called my doctor, who instructed me to go the emergency room. A tiny Chinese doctor met me. My doctor had contacted her in advance. She told me the fix was easy, a blood patch. A nurse would take several vials of blood from me and then the doctor would inject it into my spinal column. I asked the doctor how much blood she would need to inject. She said, "Oh, you tell me" in a strong Chinese accent.

Beth stood by my side and held my hand as a nurse took several vials of blood. Beth kept reassuring me it was all going to be fine as my agonizing headache was crushing me. The tiny doctor told me to lay on my side. Beth gasped as she saw the doctor take a syringe with a very large needle and fill it with my blood.

"Oh God," she said, as the doctor came closer. "Are you going to stick that in his spine?"

I squeezed Beth's hand firmly. "Beth, it's going to be OK. She knows what she's doing. She's going to make me better, I promise."

With that, the doctor stuck the large needle into my spinal column and began injecting my blood into it. At some point my headache magically just disappeared. I told her so and she said, "All done!" and withdrew the needle.

It was a really simple but effective cure. The bad news was that I would next be scheduled to meet with another neurosurgeon to discuss having a shunt put into my brain, to control the excess pressure in my skull.

My neurologist referred me to the neurosurgeon. I would go into the hospital and first have what was called "the bolt" implanted into my skull. I would remain in intensive care for three days with "the bolt" in my skull while they monitored the pressure inside my head continuously. It was to determine if I really needed the shunt.

The surgery to place the device in my skull went fine. As I lay in the ICU with my head shaved, my face swollen from the surgery, and a large tube sticking out of the top of my skull, I wondered how many of the women who were so hot to screw me in the past would want me now.

Unfortunately, and even though I was heavily sedated in ICU, I somehow pulled the bolt out of my skull. A nurse came in to check on me. I was pretty well drugged up but I recall the shock on her face. In a matter of minutes, a surgical team was putting me under to do an emergency surgery to re-implant the device into my skull right there in the ICU. I guess leaving an exposed hole showing your gray matter isn't a good thing. Later, I learned that my readings indicated that my pressure was indeed too high, and I needed a shunt after all.

At the end of the third day in ICU, I was taken back to the operating room where they put the shunt deep inside my brain with a drain running into my abdomen. I ended up with a funky-looking lump on my head about the size of half a walnut. The shunt was adjustable and the settings could be changed with a magnetic device placed over the top of the lump on my head. It was really sexy shit. It was a good thing I had a good, thick head of hair that covered it up. I was again happy that Beth had good insurance through the State of Georgia.

Beth and I had a vacation planned on the West Coast long before Ann's internship and the loss of my job had ever occurred. Shunt and all, we decided to go ahead and take the trip in advance of me getting totally focused on starting my new company. We would try to decompress a little and enjoy some time together. We'd start in San Francisco and work our way down the coastline, eventually meeting Ann in northern LA where she would still be, wrapping up her internship.

After a few days in San Francisco, Beth and I rented a car and started down Coastal 1, also known as the Pacific Coast Highway. It runs within view of the ocean for 655 miles from San Francisco to Santa Monica. The views were spectacular—well, for about the first eight hours. We figured out pretty quickly that the winding road that went through every little beach town was going to take us forever to get to Santa Barbara, where we wanted to spend a few days. We eventually bailed for Interstate 5. It wasn't scenic, but we'd get to our destination a lot quicker.

Santa Barbara was worth it. We had a room in a little laid-back, art-deco style motel a short walk from the beach, in "downtown" as much as there was a downtown, and it was relaxing. We absolutely loved Santa Barbara. As we browsed small boutiques, Beth turned to me and said, "It has the same laid-back feel as Aspen."

"Yeah, too bad someone else isn't paying our tab this time." I replied.

"You know, that's OK. It is just you and me. We're here together. No pressures, no expectations, and no schedule except to be in LA in three days. I'm kind of liking it."

Beth smiled. "You know what else? Despite all the crap you've put me through, I still kind of like you, too."

I was a bit taken back. Beth really wasn't one to be light-hearted that much, but her mood was playful and cheerful. We walked hand in hand for a while and I stopped, looking her directly in the eyes.

"I'm sorry," I said. "I'm sorry for all the times I hurt you."

"You damn well better be, you jerk!" she laughed back at me. "You owe me a lifetime of payback. I shall always get my way for as long as we live. Got it?"

"Oh shit, I better hope I don't live as long as my grandma. I think she's ninety-eight now."

We both laughed and I pulled her close for a kiss. We went into a little surf shop and Beth picked out a long-sleeve T-shirt for me, off the clearance rack, of course. She always loved a bargain. Later as we walked the beach, Beth picked up a stone about the size of an egg worn smooth by the tumbling of the Pacific waves. When we got back to the room, she wrote "Santa Barbara 2009" on it. I think she wanted something to remind her of the good times we had there. We had reconnected our souls there, again, patching up some still-sore wounds. Santa Barbara was laid back and had been good for both of us.

Santa Barbara turned out to be good for us financially, as well. I have no idea why, but while we were there, I got a call from a person in the Affirmation HR department, telling me that my severance package had been increased by $30,000. It wasn't as if I had been protesting the amount of my severance.

I'd looked at a used Harley Davidson Road King before we'd left Georgia. I decided I'd buy it after all once we got back. For a guy who wasn't having the best luck in hanging onto jobs, I was pretty flush with cash, thanks to the LJ&C settlement and a few generous severance packages.

We had a nice visit with our daughter in LA, where she gave us a tour of the RocketTech production facility. It was odd to see a major manufacturing plant right there in "the valley," as they called the area in which RocketTech was located. Yes, it was the same valley as the home of the infamous "valley girls" of 1980s and 1990s lore. Big, blond hair and ditzy was the stereotype. Ann told us many stories of how she'd get hit on by the young, skinny, California guys who dreamed of being computer game developers, or by the older, overly tanned men flaunting their wealth at the local bars. They'd see a blond, busty young woman and give it their best, but it would all go to hell when she'd tell them she was a rocket scientist. They'd laugh at first, and then she would start talking about the thermodynamic flow of rocket fuel through titanium lines feeding booster engines...and the men would slink away with their tails between their legs, defeated. No one in the valley was a match for Ann. Brains won over bravado every time.

Summer came to a close and Ann returned home for her final year at Georgia Tech. I was working to get my company some clients. I had in mind a product I'd sell. I'd developed a unique insurance product for the sub-prime auto finance market while at Affirmation. I'd used the same concept at LJ&C for their largest client. Conceptual proof had been done twice on two pretty good-sized, sub-prime auto finance companies. The Affirmation client was servicing just over 40,000 loans. The one I'd left behind at LJ&C serviced over 100,000 accounts. I knew it worked. I just needed an insurance company that would let me liberally use their non-standard auto insurance filings to bend around my needs to comply to the needs of the product.

It was a balancing act. In common terms, I had a program that was a very inexpensive tool for keeping sub-prime auto finance customers in compliance with the insurance requirement of the loan. It was just a little hard for an insurance commissioner to wrap his or her head around what I tried to explain it to them. I used a tiny portion of a company's comprehensive and collision coverage and "backed" into a flat rate that each borrower without their own insurance would pay per month. It was the bare-bones coverage required in every standard auto-lending contract, saying the borrower with provided comprehensive and collision coverage protected the lender's interest in the collateral securing the loan, or, in other words, the car. The bare-bones coverage required by the lender did not require that the borrower could file a claim. It only meant that if the lender repossessed the car and it had damage, the policy would cover the lender's loss. No such coverage was available to buy, but I had come up with such a program. For only $40 a month, an otherwise uninsured borrower got to keep the car, and the lender got the protection that was demanded through the lending contract. I was a genius. No shit—I really was, at least on this one.

I found a good-sized insurance company in

Jacksonville, FL that had heard of me and had heard that I was looking for a company. I travelled down from Atlanta and pitched them on my concept. They liked it and I had an insurance company to back my program. All I needed was clients and a computer system upon which to process the business. Oh, and I'd need staff to do data entry and customer service calls. Oh, and someone to handle accounting. I hated accounting and I was not good at it. *One step at a time, though,* I told myself. *Get a client first and then figure the rest of the shit out as you go on.* W.C Fields, the misanthropic, hard-drinking egotist comedian from the late 1930s, was unfairly given credit for the line "If you can't dazzle them with brilliance, baffle them with bull." I'd have to start making sales calls selling Owens.B Consulting using a lot of bull because there was not much brilliance in place, yet.

As I was trying to get a prospect list started for Owens.B Consulting, I got a phone call from SureTrac Software that had been sued by Excit Software when I worked there. I knew the people in charge from many, many years ago in the industry but had not directly spoken to them in a very long time. They wanted my testimony in the court case against the large oil company that had acquired Excit Softare and had never dropped the case against them. It was a total crock of bull and I told them I would be happy to help them.

As usual it started with a deposition. A date was set up in Atlanta. I was ready for what was about to happen. The deposing attorneys were there to make me look incompetent. I'd been down this road before, but I don't think they knew it. The opening lines of questions were the basics of where I'd lived, my education, where I'd worked, the basic historical stuff. They were trying to build a case that I had changed jobs a lot. It wasn't uncommon in that time period. Some of my jobs I'd been at between seven to eleven years, some had gone away in six months. I'd always been given generous severance packages. A good severance package is a sign that you had done a good job, but that the company just couldn't keep you. Otherwise, you were just shown the door and given a swift kick out with your last paycheck in hand.

They went through my employment history up to my employment at Excit Software. Then came the meaty question: "Mr. Owens, can you explain to us why you were terminated from Excit Software?"

I said, "I had been badly hurt in a motorcycle accident over one weekend and I don't know exactly why my employment was ended. I received a call while a neurologist was examining me, and I had sustained a serious concussion. I still have no memory of the event."

It was the truth. They pulled out what looked like company records and began citing rank and verse from my performance record that I had not met expectations and therefore was fired. I let them ramble on for a moment.

I asked, "Is it was customary for employees that have been terminated for non-performance to be given a large severance package?"

They scoffed at my question until I brought out the letter that had been attached to my paperwork and included the check stub for the $30,000 severance. The letter praised my performance and advised me that should I ever want to return to the firm after my recovery, a job would be waiting. They both read the letter over and had the stenographer stop for a recess. They realized their client had fucked them over. Upon resuming, they quickly wrapped up questioning. It was not going to be pretty if I had to be in the courtroom.

OWENS B LLC

Starting a company from scratch gives you a unique perspective. If you make it at some point, you can look every employee in the eye and say, "Yes, I did do your job once." I don't care if it was data entry, taking customer service phone calls, pulling staples out of papers so the document can be scanned, or cleaning the toilet. Over the years, I had done all of it. Taking the firm and reconfiguring it to be an insurance tracking company wasn't a huge step. I just had to build everything.

The first thing I did was to call Sherry Marks, the president of SureTrac Software in Texas. Her court case against Excit Software was pending a trial date, but I knew their insurance tracking software was good. I also felt really good about their chance of winning in court. They cut me a good deal on their software that based the price on the volume I ran through it. This allowed me to use it even if I signed up a small client first with no monthly minimum. I don't know if it was a favor or not but I ran with the deal. I had a software system. All I needed was accounting, operations, customer service, and, well, clients.

I decided if I started with a few small clients, I could do data entry myself in the evening and over the weekend. I would have to convince any clients I first brought on that they would have to handle their own customer service phone calls. I could give them access to a scaled-back information screen that was easy to read and understand the flow of insurance documents and letters that my firm had sent out warning of their insurance lapse. It would have to work.

I came across a perfect test case. It was a small buy-here, pay-here auto dealer/finance company in Tampa, FL. Their clients were predominately Spanish-speaking and paid their bill at the dealership where they bought the used car. Juan Vasquez owned the small operation, Vasquez Auto Sales. I got him signed up and I was officially in business. He was comfortable taking any calls from his customers generated from the insurance letter. Hell, he wanted to talk to most of them about delinquent payments anyhow.

Once a week he sent me a package of insurance documents his customers had supplied him. Over the weekend I was easily able to get all of them entered into my system. The system was programmed to produce warning letters we had printed one side in English and the other in Spanish. Lucky for me, two-sided laser printers were not crazy expensive. They were not very fast, but they were good enough for an account with only about a thousand loans on the books. More than anything Juan was a resume item for me, a reference to give to the next prospect. If you had no references, you really had a tough time getting someone to be your first. If you had one client, everyone assumed that you had figured out what you were doing and must be OK. I had a great reputation in my industry, but now I was completely on my own.

The neighborhood I lived in had a tennis team and I was an avid player. At the time Atlanta had the world's largest tennis league, called ALTA. It stood for Atlanta Lawn Tennis Association. No one played on grass. Ninety-nine percent of all the games were played on hard courts, though an occasional neighborhood had clay courts. Soon after I started Owens.B Consulting, LLC., ALTA had about 70,000 members.

Tennis was a big social thing on the Atlanta scene. My team had a very attractive, young blond woman on our team who was also a damn good player. When we played mixed doubles, I always hoped to get paired with Samantha. Sam could hold a game with most any guy. Even if she was over-matched against some lunkhead in a mixed doubles match, she did not back down. She had grit. She knew I liked her as much for her tennis skills as her attitude.

I found out Sam was studying accounting in college. I asked her if she would be interested in a part-time job as my accounting manager. She was truly flattered I would think to ask and accepted without knowing what I'd pay. I asked if she would be comfortable working out of my home as I did not have a brick-and-mortar office yet. She said she'd have no issues with it. I was thrilled I now had a client, operations (me), accounting (Sam), and an operating system from SureTrac.

I started marketing to more clients as I taught Sam about my business. We'd played tennis together for a few years now, but I really didn't know that much about her as a person. I knew she was pretty, blond, and had a very nice figure. I'd gotten into trouble with such women in the past, but somehow I knew there would be no issues working with her one-on-one alone in my home. I had a business to run and she was my head of accounting and that was it. She knew nothing about the insurance industry in general and my niche was even more remote. The concept that we billed our clients and then allowed them time to collect from their clients before reporting the premiums to the insurance carrier seemed awkward to her. It was unique to my product line.

"Beth, I've hired Sam as my accounting manager," I told my wife one evening. "Well, part-time anyhow. She'll be coming over to the house occasionally to get work and review the books with me. Are you going to be alright with this?"

"Are you planning on screwing her?" she playfully asked.

"Ah, no. I thought we might be able to fix her up with Forrest, though. You know Forrest. He plays on the men's team and does some handyman work for Christine across the street."

"I know Sam. She's way out of your league anyhow, bucko. She wouldn't stoop low enough to do you," she laughed.

And so it was. Beth was comfortable with Sam working one-on-one with me alone at our home. It was a testament to the progress we'd made in repairing our relationship.

Sam and I had been spending a lot of time together. We'd agreed on a pay scale, and I always rounded up whatever hours she reported a week. Though occasionally she worked from my house, she did a lot of the work from her dormitory. I offered to take her to lunch one day while she was over picking up some documents. I wanted to pick her brain about Ann.

We sat in a booth and, over tacos, I lamented to Sam about my daughter having a hard time finding decent guys to date. Ann had graduated from Georgia Tech and had accepted a job offer from RocketTech—the same RocketTech where she had interned the summer before. Earlier that year, Beth and I had helped Ann pack up all of her IKEA® furniture into a U-Haul® truck, hitched up a trailer to tow the new car we'd bought her for graduation, and took an epic trip from Atlanta across the southern US to move her to northern LA. (Who knew it snowed in June in New Mexico?) Anyhow, I told Sam, it seemed like Ann was never going to find a boyfriend out west.

Sam asked if she had tried a certain dating app. I said

Ann didn't like that app as it did not provide service to gay people, and she, therefore, albeit not gay, was protesting the use of it. Sam looked at me with those lovely blue eyes and shiny blond hair and said, "That's not true. I found my girlfriend on that site."

She continued on, telling me that she was a lesbian and that I was the first person outside of her immediate family or past dates that she had come out to. I sat for a moment trying to take everything in that I thought I'd just heard. Then, I went to the other side of the booth and gave her a long hug. Somehow, I had known there was a reason Sam felt more like a daughter to me than an employee or a pretty young woman I'd want to screw.

"How did your family take the news, Sam?" I asked after the hug.

"Well, my mom and sister seemed to know all along. My dad…well, my dad was crushed. He kind of disowned me."

"Have you gotten back on track with him yet?" I couldn't imagine not accepting my daughter, no matter gay or straight. I just wanted her to have someone she could share her life with.

"No, you've become my surrogate dad," Sam joked.

"Well, I am honored to have the role, and I will take it seriously. Now tell me about your girlfriend."

We continued to talk about her girlfriend, a federal agent, for a long time that afternoon, and we strengthened a bond between us that would go on forever.

Before I could get too deep into marketing, I was subpoenaed to appear in federal court in the Excit Software Inc. v. SureTrac Software Inc. case. In reality it was a giant oil company with a tiny software division going up against a little firm of about a half dozen employees.

About halfway through the hearing, I got called to the stand. Excit's attorneys had only a few questions for me and wanted me off the witness stand as fast as possible. As soon as the Excit attorney finished with me, I relaxed and settled in to begin telling my story through the questions of the SureTrac attorney. By the time I was finished, the Excit attorneys knew they had no chance at a win.

I left the stand as a recess was called for the day. Sherry, the president of SureTrac, came over and simply said, "If you ever need anything, we will take care of you."

I knew it wasn't a payoff. It was just a promise for what I had done to pay it forward. Like the little old lady in the Kentucky Fried Chicken in Greenville, I had done what was right that day.

The trial went on for a few more days. At one point, Rory Littlewood approached Sherry, offering to sell her what was left of Excit Software and drop the case. She laughed and told him, "Why buy it when I'll just take all your business away?"

I guess Littlewood's Scottish temper got the best of him and he had to be restrained. The case against SureTrac was thrown out by the judge with warnings to Excit that they were lucky to not be facing federal criminal charges for their actions.

Shortly after the trial, I learned Rory Littlewood was dead. The official ruling was suicide. The unofficial word in south Texas was that the oil company had caught him embezzling from them. He had been embezzling from the first day he had started at Excit as the president. He had been embezzling at the last firm he was with as well and had quietly gotten terminated. He had agreed to repay the money he'd embezzled if they did not press charges. He was embezzling from Excit Software to repay the last employer. Rumor was the oilmen who owned Excit Software were not happy and had him killed.

I got back to marketing. I had to go sell more accounts. I happened to catch a break when a finance company in

Chicago answered my sales calls. They were big, servicing over 40,000 sub-prime loans. In that space, that was a big lender. An enterprising young man named Jesse Fox owned the company. I looked up a few more prospects in the Chicago area and set up appointments. I was traveling on my nickel, so I had to maximize every trip. No more staying at expensive hotels; Fairfield Inns® was all I could afford.

Jesse and I hit it off right away. He understood my concept of minimizing the cash output for the insurance program and loved it. It did not take too long before his firm became my largest client. I was doing a lot of data entry in the evenings and on the weekends for his business. I was starting to have issues focusing on the data entry work, though. I started transposing numbers frequently, which I just blamed on my lack of keying skills. I had to do a lot of review of my work, more than it should have required. The small mental errors were costing me a lot of time making corrections.

As part of my marketing strategy, I decided to attend the biggest conference for the non-prime auto finance in Las Vegas. Jesse would be there as he was very involved in several industry groups. I arranged a dinner with him at one of the most expensive steakhouses in Las Vegas. It was high-end and exactly the kind of place Jesse would love. They specialized in a bone-in rib eye that had to be at least sixteen inches long. I got huge points from Jesse for that dinner. He clearly knew I was a professional in the business and willing to treat my precious clients like they mattered.

The conference went well, and I made a lot of good contacts to call upon. The bad news was that I was having a difficult time remembering the names of the people I'd met. In addition to missing names, I found myself frequently getting lost in the large hotel and the maze-like casino. It seemed as if every Las Vegas hotel makes their guests walk through the casino to get to anywhere else. I constantly got lost trying to get back to my room. Thankfully, Sam was holding down the data entry work while I travelled, in addition to her accounting duties. Beth was teaching and was not available to come with me on this trip. We really didn't want to spend the cash for both us to be traveling to the conference anyhow. We'd seen how easily cash comes and goes, and Beth and I were doing everything we could to conserve it, especially in the middle of a business start-up.

I added another smaller client, and revenues were starting to get to the level where I could afford to take a modest salary for myself. It had been a long time since I had been able to have a salary, and I felt like things were moving in the right direction until one night I stood up and immediately passed out. Beth had already gone to bed. I came to in a large puddle of blood as I had hit my head on the way down on the corner of our granite kitchen countertop. I woke her up rather woozy and asked her to look at what I thought was a scratch on my head. She was startled, to say the least. She wrapped a towel around my head and whisked me off to the emergency room.

Fourteen staples later, they had my head closed up. No one seemed too concerned about how or why my fall had happened. I must have tripped in the dark, I reassured myself. I had yet another concussion.

It wasn't until the same event occurred a few months later when this time, I awoke to find myself laying in a puddle of blood again and realized that I had also lost my bowels. I went straight to the shower to clean myself up before waking Beth and showing her the wound. It was almost exactly where I'd lacerated my head open before. This time, when I got to the emergency room a nurse took my blood pressure. A normal reading is somewhere around 120/80. I was at about 40/10. The attending doctor said to forget the staples, and they started putting IV needles into every vein they could find to push fluids and meds into me to get my pressure up before I died. Once they got the blood pressure up to an acceptable level, they went back to work stapling the wound. This time I was referred to my neurosurgeon. They thought the shunt was not working. Beth suggested seeing a neurologist instead.

I fought the idea of seeing a neurologist, but Beth was insistent. I had a fledgling company to grow, I pointed out to her. I had no time to be down. I did sales all day and keyed data half the night and on the weekends. If I traveled, I took data entry with me that I worked on in the hotel in the evenings. There were no more expensive and late-night prospect dinners. I did my sales calls during business hours. If the prospect wanted an after-hour drink or a visit to a strip club, that was going to be on their nickel. First off, I couldn't afford that way of doing business anymore and second, I'd done it too many times before. The biggest abusers of the vendor expense account did not always buy. These day, I vowed, if I were going to stuff twenty-dollar bills into a G-string, I'd beg my wife to get one instead and role-play for me. At least then I could make love to her at the end of the show.

Still, the appointment with the neurologist came. I was having pretty bad headaches regularly but attributed them to stress. He wanted to do an MRI. Beth and I were shocked at the results.

I had a rare neurological condition named Chiari Malformation. It basically means your brain is too big for your skull and is pushing out the bottom of the skull. Why wasn't this seen before, when I had been treated for the tumor?

The condition impacts all type of body functions, including balance, memory, and bowel functions. Because the symptoms are so diverse, many people have varied degrees of the condition and are never correctly diagnosed. They go to their doctor with an incontinence problem. The urologist looks at everything related to the kidneys and bladder and finds nothing. They tell the patient there is nothing wrong with them when in fact the brain is pressing on a portion of itself that controls the bladder. When they turn their head the wrong way or get a bump to the head, they piss themselves. The same is true for the lower bowel. It is embarrassing for people who get called hypochondriacs when there actually is a very real neurological explanation to their symptoms.

Most doctors don't think to do an MRI for a bowel problem. The problem severity is measured in how many millimeters your cerebellum, the lower part of the brain, has hemorrhaged out of your skull and is pressed into your upper spine. A mild case could be three to four millimeters. I was at eleven millimeters. Severe.

Beth and I once again began researching neurosurgeons. There was an expert in Denver and another in New York, but as luck would have it, the head of neurosurgery who had been in my brain before was considered one of the best in this rare field as well.

I went straight to him. He looked at my MRI for about fifteen minutes.

"Kevin, based on what I see here, you have maybe four months to live. The malformation of your skull is squeezing your brain into your spinal column. It is choking the spinal fluid off, essentially drying your brain out. A lot of damage had already been done and I need to get you into surgery quickly."

There was no sarcasm this time. He reminded me that actual brain surgery was painless. The bad news was that this was the most painful kind of brain surgery. He would have to cut all of my neck muscles off my skull to rebuild it. He would also be reforming the top two vertebrae. Once he rebuilt the shape of my skull to accommodate my brain, he and his surgical team would reattach my neck muscles. The shunt would come out at the same time. He didn't

dance around it: recovery would be hell.
I would be in surgery a few days later

I had a lot to do. I had a company to run. I had to somehow make preparations to keep it running while I was out of commission. I reached out to Sherry at SureTrac. She had said they would take care of me, and they were not kidding. They offered to take over all of my data entry until whenever I was up to taking it back. They would also run my weekly processing cycles. They also let me know that they had been banking commission on an account I had brokered their software for years ago. They would pay me the commission so I had extra money for hospital expenses while I was down. She told me that my testimony killed the lawsuit against them. It had allowed them to move their business forward. These were good people and I was ever so proud to be associated with them.

I called my clients and told them I was sick. I gave them the details of my condition. I also gave them the details of my back-up plan. They were all comfortable with what I had put together, all the phone numbers, emails address, and so on, including my wife's, for everyone. I told them my wife would call them the day of surgery and let them know I survived, assuming I had survived. This was a very intense surgery with big risks. Jesse was the most supportive of all the clients. He was really most caring about how I was going to fare. In the near future, I would become a fundraiser for an organization doing research for Chairi Malformation. Jesse Fox would become my largest donor. The organization recognized me as one of the top ten fundraisers in the country that year.

Sam had her instructions to send all the insurance documents to SureTrac data entry, and I was ready to get a "zipper." People who had the corrective surgery for Chiari

Malformation were known as "zipperheads," thanks to the eleven-to-twelve-inch cut made at the crown of their skull running down to the base of their neck. This cut was stapled closed in such a way that it took on the look of a long zipper running down the back of someone's head.

Beth and I made the trip back to Emory for a repeat at the neurosurgical pre-op unit. This time our arrival was closer to 5:00 am, and their pre-op area was under construction. It wasn't quite as impressive as round one. The surgery was just as long. I think I was on the table between eleven to twelve hours. Maybe the neurosurgical team bills by the hour and that is why they went so slow. I suppose when you are taking a person's skull apart and reforming it and reassembling it to fit that person's brain, you have to take your time. It is more art than science. The surgeon knows the skull needs to be bigger, but until he cracks open the skull and the brain pops out, as the neurosurgeon described before the operation, he doesn't know how much space he'll actually need to make. Once he figures that part out, he gets to figure out how to make it all go back together, all in the meantime without damaging the brain. No wonder neurosurgeons have huge egos.

My mother had come down from Tennessee to be with us the day of the surgery. After surgery I felt like shit and asked for something for pain. They gave me some pills, which I promptly threw back up. I was lying there with two IV lines and they were giving me pain pills. I do give my mom some credit for the way she took care of me then. The little old lady jumped into the face of one of the nurses and demanded an IV pain med. A call was made and, in a minute, I was enjoying Dilaudid®, the most powerful painkiller available. I slept through the night.

I lived through the surgery. Beth got to leave late-night messages for family, friends, and clients that I had survived. The nursing staff was very liberal with the Dilaudid. I think the neurosurgical ICU recovery nurses must have known how painful that particular surgery was. They kept the good stuff coming from the start. I dreaded the day I would be discharged and would no longer be able to get that dose of Dilaudid shot into my IV for immediate pain relief. When it came to pain meds, through the many orthopedic procedures I'd endured, I never even get close to becoming addicted. But Dilaudid made me understand how people could get addicted. If I had had an unlimited supply of that stuff, I would have been pushing it in constantly. Thankfully the nurses cut me off once I got discharged and I had to live with oral pain meds, which I took as few as possible. I disliked the way they made me feel. I didn't sleep well when taking them and they made my skin itch.

As my health improved, I slowly started keying some documents. SurTrack insisted they could keep doing them. I just sent a little less each week. I wasn't going to milk their charity forever. My head was healing up and I was re-engaging in the business world.

One of the items on my agenda was a large sub-prime auto finance conference in Orlando coming up. I decided to go to it and try to make new contacts. The date came and I decided to take a flight, as I didn't think I could handle the drive with my neck not yet fully recovered. My staples were out by then, but the zipper line was still fresh on the back of my head. Some hair had grown in, but not too much. As I sat in one of the sessions I had a particular interest in, I noticed a guy a few years younger than me who wore his head shaved. He had a zipper line down his head.

As the session ended, I went up to him and said, "By chance, are you a zipperhead?"

He simply smiled a big smile and responded, "If you

know what one is, that tells me something."

I turned around, revealing the back of my head. We had a good laugh and talked about our common condition for a few minutes.

"Hi, I am Kevin Owens. Zipper date: 6/21/11."

"Ben Gaylord. Zipper date: 2/19/09. I own Rápido Finance in Chicago."

Talk surrounded our common neurological condition for a while but we did eventually move to the business side of things. He owned a medium-size auto finance company that actually competed against my largest client. I asked him if I could set up a sales call, to which he agreed. It was the start of a good relationship with Ben.

My first official sales call with Ben in Chicago was fascinating. Like myself, he was a BMW driver, except he drove really high-end BMWs. During my first visit to his office complex, Ben asked me, "Would like to see my garage?"

I was being polite, as I assumed the building had a parking garage. "Sure, let's take a look at it, if you have time."

We went to the center of the building, which opened up into a huge space. It turned out Ben had this little thing for Porsches, too. He raced them. He specifically bought that building so that he could build a garage in the center of it for his two race Porsche 911s. It had a lift, a space for the trailer to take them to the racetrack and tools, lots of tools.

"Ben, you are seriously into this, aren't you?" I stammered.

"I think of it as a really expensive hobby."

I drooled over this incredible set up. He took time to show me the two 911s that were built specifically for track use. These were not street-legal cars. They had full roll cages and all the professional instruments any racecar would have in them. No doubt, I was envious. Despite that

I was doing business with his key competitor, we came to terms, and Ben became my second largest client. It was great news for me, but I now officially had more volume than I could personally ever handle. I had to either get a business loan to establish an operations center or find a firm that I could outsource my operations to until I added more revenue to support a brick-and-mortar office and staff. I was almost there, but not quite.

I had a good relationship with Jesse, and I talked to him about investing in my firm. I let him know that it was growing and I needed to either outsource some functions or open an operations center. He said he wasn't interested in investing but knew someone who could be a good business partner for me.

Joseph Willard owned an insurance company based in Chicago and had done business with Jesse over the past several years. Introductions were made over a dinner in Chicago and we talked about outsourcing data entry and customer service phone calls to his operations center. I told him I would put in a financial offer for our work together.

Insurance guys like Mr. Willard were easy for me to understand. We spoke the same language, premium and commission. I structured a processing deal based on the volume of premium my firm generated that was a cut of my commission. He understood what I was doing and liked the offer. We quickly came to terms as my new client Ben was just coming up. It was a good thing, as the initial mailing to Ben's clients was enormous. Ben had never tracked insurance records for his clients before. We pretty much had to send all of his borrowers a soft notification to send in their proof of insurance that had originally been required when they took out their automobile loan.

Phone calls came in on almost every letter that went out. Sub-prime borrowers were not the nicest callers. They were used to the lender calling them because they were behind in their payments, threating to repossess their car. Any contact with the lender was usually hostile in nature. The borrowers did not know who they were calling as the letter just said "Insurance Center" at the bottom and had their lender's name on the top. It was a rough start-up, but at the point where we had about sixty percent of the borrowers data into the system, we decided to pull the plug and start issuing insurance policies and charging borrowers. Willard was happy as it meant premium would finally be written and commissions would start being paid. Mr. Willard would be getting paid for all the work he'd been doing for free. He knew the deal going in, but I don't think he really understood what he was getting into despite my warnings.

With Mr. Willard's team doing my processing, I had time to get back to sales and marketing. My budget was tight, as I had had to cut my salary to pay Mr. Willard's team. Focusing on growing the company was paramount. I had to really double my existing size to open my own operations center. I was working the market as hard as I could when Mr. Willard approached me with an idea to become actual business partners. He wanted to buy the company from me. His insurance company sold regular automobile insurance and sold automobile insurance to sub-prime customers such as Jesse Fox's. He had this idea that if he knew which customers of Fox's were uninsured, his team could reach out to them just before getting the lender-placed policy that they'd be forced to pay and successfully sell them regular insurance.

I had been down this road many years before when I worked for a large insurance company in Cleveland, Ohio. It was the reason that company got into the lender-place insurance market. It failed miserably. I tried and tried to explain to Mr. Willard that one of the premier auto insurance companies in the country had tried and failed at this approach. But he scoffed at me, saying his team was far more talented than anyone at the Cleveland firm had at selling insurance.

On the other hand, I was running out of short-term capital and did not want to start pulling funds out of the money I'd reinvested into my retirement savings. We had done that before when times were tough and I was trying hard to get caught up. We started talking about the valuation of my company.

Insurance firms are tough to value. Customers bought their insurance from the key people at an insurance agency. There are no tools or raw material or stock to value in the transaction. I did not own a building or have staff. I was basically leasing Mr. Willard's staff. If I sold all or the majority interest to him, I would be the president of the firm with a set salary. I would have a five-year contract. I could focus on sales and marketing, my area of expertise. I'd have a bonus program that rewarded me for growing the company.

Beth and I had long and difficult discussions about the option. She knew how hard I'd worked to get the company off the ground after the last corporate disappointment. She had also watched me fight back after a second brain surgery to keep working when I should have taken at least three months to recover. I had been back at work within two weeks. I would also be part of a larger insurance conglomerate. Mr. Willard had an insurance company and about forty insurance agencies spread out over Illinois, Michigan, Indiana, and Wisconsin. I didn't like the answer, but it was becoming clear. The best thing for my family and me was to sell.

We agreed to a price and set up a dinner in Chicago to sign papers and toast the deal. Mr. Willard would take full ownership of the company.

Beth flew up to Chicago to join us for the celebration of the business sale, as did Mr. Willard's second wife, Sophia. She was a very attractive woman and clearly, I thought, she was a trophy wife. Joseph Willard wasn't an ugly old geezer, but the second wife was clearly a very attractive younger woman when he married her and she had aged well. As we ate our steaks, Mr. Willard gushed about how smart she was and how she had an MBA from a prestigious university.

I wasn't sure where it was all going until he said, "Sophia will be the CEO of the company. You will report directly to her."

I knew at that point I'd been screwed over.

Sophia's first official function as CEO was to rename the company. As part of the purchase agreement, I retained the legal rights to the name Owens.B Consulting., LLC. The Willard's didn't want this name, though, since it reflected my identity. Sophia came up with the name Synapsis, Inc. To me it sounded like a medical term, but it wasn't my company anymore. If she wanted to name an insurance tracking firm after the fusion of chromosome pairs, that was up to her. I suspected she had no idea what the definition of the term was when she suggested it.

The incident reminded me of a woman I met back in college when I was working at the hospital. She had named her daughter after the technical term for a baby's first bowel movement. When a nurse asked her about the name, the woman said she'd heard it and thought it was pretty. I felt bad for a girl going through life named "Meconium" and having to explain to people what her name meant. I bet at some point someone gave her the nickname "Lil' Shit."

The first official Synapsis, Inc. function was a conference in Las Vegas. I was happy it was not on my dime. We would not have a company booth as we did not have time to get graphics made up for it. Instead, we would attend seminars and work the crowd trying to meet as many prospects as possible. We invited Ben out to dinner as well.

We set up reservations at the same expensive steakhouse again. It was still one of the more impressive restaurants in Las Vegas. This time, I took Beth with me to the conference, on my dime. She had never been to Las Vegas and I was tired of spending nights alone in hotel rooms. I must have spent at least a thousand nights in hotels alone over the years. I wasn't going to do it anymore. Beth could wander the conference crowd with me as my guest and listen to my boring company spiel a hundred times if she could stand it. She went to the dinner with Ben and was truly impressed, if not embarrassed, by the tomahawk rib eye steak I ordered. We got a good photo out of the event. Like Jesse, Ben was impressed with the restaurant. But it was different with Ben. I think he was more appreciative that I made the trip and spent the money on him with our limited budget. He knew he wasn't our largest client, but that night I made him feel like he was the most important one. We'd struck a bond that would continue for many years. Maybe it was the same large scar on the back of our heads, maybe it was being the "little guy" in a big market, but we had a connection.

Ben eventually introduced me to his neurosurgeon at the University of Illinois-Chicago who had developed an experimental device to stop headaches caused by the decompression Chari Malformation surgery. Nerves in my neck had been damaged during that surgery, and I had almost constant headaches. His neurosurgeon had come up with a use of a neurostimulator implanted in the cerebellum to stop pain signals traveling to the rest of the brain. It would be my third brain surgery to have the device implanted.

Working with Sophia Willard was challenging. OK, she was a complete idiot when it came to business. She was a very good-hearted but spoiled, rich woman. She complained to me if the auto dealer didn't return her Range

Rover to the exact same parking spot in her Chicago high rise-condo after a technician had picked it up for an oil change, but then she would tip the delivery driver $50. She was nice to the waiters at Morton's Steakhouse but then moaned to me if they were slow in bringing her salad to the table. She'd tip them $100 for an $80 dinner just to, I think, flash the money. She wore jewelry that was worth more than my car. She thought the world was there to please her. Her high-rise condo overlooked Lake Michigan and yet she complained she had no money. When we would travel to do sales calls, I was expected to carry our entire luggage into the hotels and up to the room. I was expected to pump the gas into the car even if it was her car. It was as if I was a hired servant.

This was bullshit and I was sick of it. When I talked to her husband about the crap I was dealing with, he would roll his eyes and say, "Wow, women, they sure can be high maintenance."

But I'd think, *What the hell?* Maybe she was high-maintenance, but this was business. It wasn't my job to babysit his bored wife. I was fed up.

Things got much worse before they would ever get better. As Willard's insurance company only sold in the states surrounding Illinois, all of our prospects were within driving distance from Chicago. I would fly in from Atlanta and meet Sophia, where we'd pick between her Range Rover, Mercedes Benz, or Maserati to drive to our appointments. I never believed in showing up to a sales call in an expensive car.

Jerry, the owner of Simon & Associates, a previous client in Buffalo, had a sweet Porsche 911. The first time I went there to do a joint sales call on a larger prospect, he picked me up from the airport in a ten-year-old Jeep Cherokee. I asked him where the Porsche was. He told me he never drove it to a client because he never wanted them to see he was making any money off them. The ten-year-old Jeep looked like basic, frugal transportation. It wasn't beat up; it was four-wheel drive, which helped in Buffalo, but in no way it said "money."

A $50,000 Range Rover screamed money. It was rubbing it in our clients' face. While Maserati's value fell like a rock from the moment you drove it off the dealer's lot, the common person still saw an exotic Italian sports sedan that they could never afford. In reality an average middle management banker could buy a three-year-old Maserati for about the same cost as a new Toyota Camry, but they didn't know it.

Plus, we showed up to sales calls habitually late. It drove me insane. I had never been late for a sales call in my life. For Sophia the world revolved around her and she showed up when she felt like it and expected people to drop whatever they were doing to meet with her. She genuinely did not understand when people were either pissed off or flat out refused the meeting because we were late. She was Sophia Willard. I'm sure she thought to herself all the time, "Who are these little people who won't drop whatever they are doing to meet with me?"

I would stand in the background, too embarrassed to say a word. My reputation was being flushed down the toilet.

The deepest insult came after making a sales call in Indianapolis. We were booked into a nice hotel. Our hotels had to have a bar because Sophia had to have a few martinis every evening. As always, I got the bags to the room and agreed to meet at the bar to discuss where we'd eat dinner and strategize on the next day's sales call. I always wanted to review everything available via the Internet about a prospect before arriving. How were their latest financial reports? Were they involved in any community events? Maybe they had acquired branches from a competitor. Any scrap of information may be of value in a sales call.

Unfortunately, Sophia was getting a bit too drunk in the bar. We opted to get some food there instead of leaving the hotel. She drank more with dinner. She got to the point where I had to help her back to her room. Upon arriving she asked me to sit tight as she had my new Apple® iPad.

She had a suite. I sat in the first portion while she went to the second room to get the device. She came back with her top unbuttoned.

She walked toward me, saying, "Honey, rub my back."

"Sophia!" I yelled instantly, standing up. "I'm a married man. This is not right!"

She laughed at me and said, "I'm not paying you to screw me. If I want that, I'll tell you when and how. Now rub my back. It hurts from driving."

She threw a bottle of some undoubtedly expensive body lotion at me and pulled off her top, thankfully leaving her bra on, and flopped down on the bed face-first. Well, that was good news. At least I wasn't going to be screwing to keep my job that day. It wasn't about anything sexual. I was nothing more than the massage therapist at the spa that day.

I put some lotion on my hands and gave her a half-assed back rub. I'd been trained at the hospital where I'd worked how to do professional back rubs. This woman was not getting my "A" game or anywhere close to it. Only my wife got my "A" game.

I finished and headed for my room. I didn't bother setting up a breakfast time. Sophia could figure it out herself. She really had no clue that an employee was not a personal servant who performed whatever service she wanted.

The next day it was as if the event in her hotel room had never happened. She didn't bring it up, and neither did I. I was totally at a loss for words. On one hand I'd seen enough women in the business world who were more than happy to screw around with co-workers. I also had a five-year contract guaranteeing me a job and salary. About the only way they couldn't pay me was if I quit. Sure, there were sexual harassment laws, but what was I going to do, claim my superior took off her top and made me rub her back? I hadn't gotten fired, I hadn't lost my job and salary, and I didn't have an ounce of proof that anything had happened. I would catch a break soon.

The shit hit the fan as we were converting data from the servers I ran my business on at SureTrac to the computer servers at Mr. Willard's company. An error occurred in the set-up for Jesse Fox's account. We didn't know it at the time, but things went wrong and over a short period of time we issued $250,000 of insurance policies that we should not have issued to his borrowers. His company had collected the money from the customers and paid it to us. These people did not need the policies. We had a glitch in the system that was not processing the insurance cancelations as they should have been done.

Just by chance, as I was walking through the operations center talking with a data entry person, I noticed an employee keying a document. I took a closer look at the screen and noticed a string of policies that caught my attention. Something didn't look right. A little bit of research turned over the error. I called my team at SureTrac and found we had issued just over a quarter million dollars in policies in error. I took the information to Sophia immediately.

"Sophia, we have a problem. The system has not been canceling the lender-placed coverage when the borrower sends in their proof of coverage."

"What are you talking about? Everything is running fine," she replied tersely.

"No, we have issued about a quarter million dollars of coverage that we should not have issued on Jesse's account."

"Are you sure?" she questioned.

"Yeah. I was going through Operations a few days ago and noticed a screen that had way too many certificates issued. I had SureTrac run some reports. We failed to set up the system properly. This is a major screw up."

"Kevin, if we fix this, will Jesse know? Will it impact his commission?" she demanded.

"Hell yeah. And not only that—you are going to have to return about fifty thousand in commission," I replied.

"Make it go away," she growled.

We had helped Jesse set up a retrospective commission agreement with our insurance carrier. It was a deal where Jesse, who was a licensed insurance agent himself, would get a cut of commission on our insurance program over the long term from the company backing the program. The insurance company liked it because Jesse had an incentive to keep his losses under control. If the losses were low, his bite of the pie would be bigger. If losses were high, he would get no pie at all. Sophia's response shocked me.

"Make the cancels go away," she repeated.

She wanted the entire mistake to be wiped from the books as if it had never happened. She was adverse to having to tell Jesse we had made a mistake. Her husband had done business with Jesse for years and she wasn't going to tell him or Jesse that we had screwed up. "Just make it all go away" were my instructions. If Mr. Willard had been caught doing what she asked me to do, he would have lost his insurance license in every state he did business in and it most likely would bankrupt him. It was insurance fraud, a felony offence.

I had to make a decision. I told her it would take special programming that SureTrac would have to do to make the transactions "go away," and since I no longer owned the company, I had no authority to ask SureTrac to do such work. If she wanted it done, she would have to ask them to do it herself. To be safe, I kept a back-up file of all the accounts that had been impacted. I also drafted my resignation letter. I was not going to work for a criminal.

I gave my resignation letter to her. "Sophia, I am not going to be a part of committing insurance fraud. I have too many years in this business to trash my reputation over a bullshit mistake."

"You can't quit. I own you. You are bought and paid for for five years," she spewed.

"No, I can quit at any time. You can be the CEO of this fine little mess you are setting up. I am not going to have anything to do with this any longer. You know where to send my final check."

I also did not want to find out if indeed at some point I was going to be told to screw her to keep my job. She saw me as a servant. I have no doubt that if she got drunk enough again one night that I would be commanded to perform.

Things got ugly.

"You little shit! If you breathe a word of what happened to anyone, we will have our attorneys eat you alive. You will be sorry you were ever born you little bastard!"

"Sophia, you can kiss my ass goodbye," I told her. "I am sick of putting up with your shit, and now I know you are a criminal, too. I am not going down with you. You will never see me again."

At that point I really didn't want to have any more to do with her or what had happened to the company I started. I'd lost my dream of running a nice little firm until I was seventy years old and selling it for a tidy sum to retire into the sunset.

I took my backup data and departed for home. I hoped I would never hear from any of the Chicago mistake again.

I decided not to mention the hotel room incident to Beth. After careful consideration, I decided no good could possibly come from telling her. It would only upset her. My reason for quitting was the fraud. I'd explain that to her, and she would understand and support my reasoning. She, of all the people I knew, believed in doing things the right way and upholding the law. She would not want her husband being a party to insurance fraud. I'd go back to independent consulting.

My old pal Ronald Mantle heard I was consulting again. Now that I was available, he wanted to hire me to come in and look at his firm. He'd basically given up running the firm years ago and just never sold it. It would be income. It wasn't my favorite role, evaluating someone else's company. But I was good at it. I had plenty of experience from a role as an internal auditor at the Cleveland insurance firm I'd worked for years ago.

I worked with Mantle for about six months. It was tough talking to his staff. Employees said they never had written job objectives, and they didn't even know who they reported to in the organization. The person heading up sales and client servicing was in her mid-seventies. She had been working for Mantle for almost forty years. I interviewed their remaining customers. The head of sales and client servicing was great at bringing donuts. While I was in my review process the largest client announced they were leaving. They were tired of getting donuts and no real service.

There really wasn't any saving Mantle's business unless he was willing to terminate his head of sales and client servicing. She was a stubborn woman who didn't know when to hang it up. Instead, she was dragging Mantle's firm down. He needed to either hire a new management team or sell the company. It was the fairest thing for his staff.

I was noticing something wasn't right as I worked to review Mantle's financials and contracts and to try to work with his head of sales on a modern marketing plan. I was having a lot of trouble maintaining my focus. I couldn't remember things. Formulas that I normally built into spreadsheets in minutes now took hours. I found when I met new people, I could not remember their names. Nothing was working right in my head.

Our daughter had taken a new job in Charlotte, North Carolina, and Beth and I decided to follow her there. We sold our house in Atlanta and moved that same year. Beth was fed up with teaching public school. We both needed a new start. My consulting work could be based from anywhere.

We rented a townhouse in a nice neighborhood and started looking at where to settle in. Beth found a job teaching at a private school. There, they taught children with learning disabilities. It was a great fit for her. She, as I learned again and again over the course of my marriage with her, has almost unlimited patience. The nice thing, too, was that her maximum class size was six students. Her school appreciated its staff and treated them well. Plus, Beth and I were happy that we were once again living near our only child.

Ann had found a boyfriend in the Charlotte area. A two-year romance turned into a destination wedding. We had lunch with Ann and her fiancé, Adam, one afternoon.

As we finished our food, she said, "We have an announcement. We're getting married!"

Beth and I were very surprised. They hadn't shown any signals about a wedding.

Ann continued on, "While Adam and I were in St. Martin walking on the beach one evening, he romantically got down on one knee, pulled out the ring, and asked me to marry him."

I turned and looked at Adam. "You know how to pick a good time and place."

"Well, I'd had it in mind for quite a while, and I'd bought the ring. I was just waiting for the right time. I wanted to make sure she'd say 'yes.'"

"Looks like you guessed right, son, or is it too soon to call you that?"

Ann turned red.

"Ah, I think I'd rather stick with Adam, if you don't mind," he said, his cheeks beginning to match Ann's.

"No, that's fine by me!" I blabbered. "Welcome to the family."

We stood up and hugged each other, and Beth and I looked at each other, beaming.

"So, do you two have plans for the wedding? How much is this going to set me back?" I joked.

"Well, Dad, considering how both Adam and I both make more a year now than you do," Ann shot back, smiling, "we'll pay for the wedding, which will be at the first port of call on the cruise we're hoping everyone in the family will be on with us."

Beth laughed and reached across the table for Ann. "Well, we are at least going to buy your wedding dress for you. You can't take the wedding dress shopping away from me."

"I was planning on you helping me pick out a dress, Mom. I also want to use your bridal veil, too!"

Ann went on, making her mom the happiest woman on the planet that day.

They married on the same Caribbean island where Beth and I had honeymooned almost thirty-eight years before— St. Thomas. Beth had a wonderful time the day of the wedding helping Ann prepare for the ceremony. They got off the ship, and a wedding planner had a hair salon set up, with make-up, flowers, and catering all arranged.

I had it easy. Adam and I enjoyed a good cigar and bourbon before the ceremony. I got to walk my little girl down a sandy aisle in my shorts, sandals, and a nice linen shirt. Beth wore a beautiful, beachy maxi dress. She was as beautiful as when we had honeymooned there all those years before.

Our daughter wore a traditional, white wedding gown, and the groom wore a tux with sandals. It was a beautiful seaside wedding. I know the mother of the bride and I could not have been happier.

While Beth and I sat at the reception, I reflected on how far different of a person I was that day than from ten years before. I felt in love with my wife. She looked magnificent with the tropical breezes blowing through her hair. Even with a small touch of gray beginning, she still had wonderful hair. She was no longer a size zero as when we'd met, but she now had a healthy size and weight. She was trim compared to most women her age and had aged ever so gracefully.

We were still sitting under the shelter in the reception area when a rain shower hit, soaking the bride and groom as they were getting photos taken. Beth and I were so worried their day would be spoiled, but we were thrilled when they joined the reception soaked and laughing.

"Beth, let me get you some champagne!" I said. "We need to celebrate this moment. It has been a long time coming."

"How much have you had to drink? She only got engaged a few months ago Kevin."

"No, it took us thirty-eight years to get here, honey. We've survived so many ups and downs. So many tough times, and here we are, still together, celebrating our daughter's joyous day."

I had tears in my eyes.

"Oh geez, your brain damage is showing, honey" Beth quietly said and gave me a kiss on the cheek.

I finally felt my life was coming together. We could spend the remainder of the trip enjoying the cruise in the

Caribbean. However, later, I could not remember who had attended the wedding. I really couldn't remember what food was served at the reception, either. I knew Beth and I were at the wedding but the details were a blur. Years ago, I would have blamed it on too many martinis, but I knew I'd only had a couple of glasses of champagne.

The next day, as I sat on a deck chair trying to recall the details of the wedding, I began to reflect on how I had gotten to be where I was that very day. I had fallen in love with Beth within minutes of meeting her and proposed to her within hours of first laying eyes upon her. It had been crazy to do so, and everyone agreed. My dad had given the marriage six months before it would end in divorce. But, here we were, thirty-eight years later, still married despite everything I'd done wrong. How had we managed to survive all of it—the infidelity, the financial ruin, and the illness? We were finding out that being married to someone with brain damage wasn't easy. I'd spent so much time away from home chasing the big money in sales. It had led me into the arms of other women that maybe a tumor caused me the inability to resist. Maybe it had just been a huge character flaw. I really didn't know. I did know how thankful I was to be there, though, right at that moment, participating in our daughter's wedding, still married to Beth.

I marveled that she had not left me. We never had a deep conversation about why she had not divorced me. I suspect I was afraid to know. If I brought it up and she thought about it, maybe she'd reconsider and throw me out. I guess I was one part thankful and another part afraid of the truth. For years, I'd felt she deserved someone better than me, that maybe she had acted impulsively the night I proposed. Yet, she had stayed with me. She had shown me time and again that she truly loved me. Why couldn't I get this through my thick head? She really did love me, despite all my flaws.

Unfortunately, the return from St. Thomas found me at a center for Alzheimer's. My neurologist thought the problems I was having processing information and remembering names was a sign of early-onset Alzheimer's. I can tell you, there is never a good day to be examined by an Alzheimer's expert to see if you have the disease. It is terrifying.

Over the years, especially around the times I'd had my brain surgeries, I had studied the disease and had read up on famous people who had shared their stories before they became incapacitated. Sitting in that office that afternoon was one of the lowest points of my life. I was not so much afraid for myself but of what the disease would do to my beloved wife. She had forgiven me for so many mistakes. She had sat in so many hospital waiting rooms as doctors had taken me apart and put me back together. She had stuck by my side when I had told her I wanted to leave. I could not imagine putting her through the hell of caring for me if I had Alzheimer's. She had always deserved better than me, and to think of her stuck with someone who wouldn't even know who she was after all I'd put her through...I would have rather taken my motorcycle out on a very fast ride off a cliff somewhere in the mountains.

We met with the team of doctors who ran me through a battery of tests. They were sure I did not have early-onset Alzheimer's. It was a relief, but what was happening? Why were my cognitive skills failing me? It would mean a trip back to my neurologist to discuss the results from the testing at the Alzheimer's clinic.

My doctor did not have particularly good news. The years of scattered injuries and surgeries to my brain had taken a serious toll. He said my short-term, or "working memory," was almost non-functional. My long-term memory was fine. My ability to process information in real-time was impaired. The calculations I used to do in my head for my business I would never be able to do again. My ability to find my way home from new places wasn't good. I would need a GPS in my car to ensure I could find my way home until I'd repeated a trip fifteen or twenty times. It would take that long for the neural path to get it into my long-term memory. I would not remember people's names until I'd been told them many times over.

I was sent to a neuro-therapist to learn how to deal with my new reality. People with severe brain damage keep trying to revert to their "old lives," he told me, despite not having the cognitive skills to lead them. It took me a year of neurotherapy to learn who the new "me" was and to gain new coping skills as to how to live day by day with minimal short-term memory.

My doctors advised me to retire. My ability to do the work, to run a company as I had done, was gone. There was too much brain damage.

I stopped consulting and applied for Social Security disability on the advice of my financial advisor. He told me it would be best not to tap into our investments or 401k money if at all possible until later in life. I was only 56. There would never be any more sex-crazed women putting me in situations where I'd make bad decisions. There also would never be a six-figure income again.

I did get approved for Social Security disability forty days after I was examined by an agency-approved doctor. All of my doctors submitted records of the brain surgeries, neurological damage, and treatments I'd received. It was a thick file. Social Security deemed me totally and permanently disabled.

At first, I thought, "Wow, only forty days. Some people wait years for approval."

Then I realized I was officially a turnip. A government stamped-and-approved turnip. Yea for me! I didn't feel depressed, but this realization was sobering.

I had to learn to rely on Beth for so much. There were simple things such as her leaving me notes each day of things to accomplish before she left for work. It kept me from just rambling around the house aimlessly.

When we went places, she was the one now who knew how to get there, not me. I had always been our compass and map.

She made lists for me when I went to the grocery store; otherwise, I'd come home missing many of the items I'd gone to get.

These changes weren't huge, monumental things, but they affected the little things that you normally do every day without thinking about them. I'd lost the ability to do a lot without ever realizing it.

I kept thinking about how I had been so cruel to her for so long, and yet she loved me. I had cheated, lied, and kidded myself at times that what I had done was justifiable or forgivable or not that bad. I was so lucky to have her.

I also thought about my professional life. I had fought so hard to climb up that corporate ladder, and for what? Only a handful of old business contacts called me now and then. Walter stayed in touch, as did Liala and Sam. Pretty much the rest of the industry moved on and forgot about me, just like some days I couldn't remember to pull up my own zipper after taking a piss. A few friends from my motorcycling days back in Georgia would text or email now and then, but now that I wasn't riding with them the contact happened less and less. Richie stayed in touch more so than anyone.

Beth would come home from work and ask what I had done that day, and I would just stare off and have no idea. What *had* I really accomplished? I suppose over the years I created employment for a fair number of people in the firms I was associated with or outright owned. My work allowed them to feed their families, pay their rent, and have healthcare coverage. I'd like to kid myself that my low-cost insurance product I'd developed helped people stay in auto loans that otherwise might have had their car repossessed, but even I knew that was a bit of a stretch. I laughed to myself, thinking, *Well, gosh, look how many airline, hotel, rental car, and restaurant employees I helped keep employed over all those years of my constant business travel!*

On a more serious note, Beth and I had created a beautiful and productive daughter. We left her with no student debt. I helped her get a job that started a lucrative engineering career. We gave her and her husband a significant gift toward the down payment of their first home. I had earned enough for us to pay cash for a nice, new house in Charlotte in a community for people fifty-five years old and up. At least most of the other resident now don't mind when I cannot remember their names.

I did finally find the salvation I had sought for so long in the simple surroundings of my home and with my wife. I didn't need to fight and climb the corporate ladder. Beth loved me even as a brain-damaged, aging guy with a meager disability income.

These days, I don't drive a new BMW every two years to impress Beth. We do have a nice, new modest SUV in the garage, and I have a sporty little Italian convertible that Beth loves to drive. I keep the house clean as Beth continues to teach special needs children. We have a manicured backyard that overlooks a wonderful wooded area. There are many days I sit out in one of our Adirondack chairs watching the birds at our feeder. I think back at the mistakes I made, the life I was living, Sonja, Donna, all of it. Why couldn't I have lost my long-term memories instead and just be living in the present? Not remembering at times would have been less painful.

I think about my inability to make rational decisions that any normal married man would have made at the time. I was living large, drinking martinis, eating at the finest restaurants, and had women wanting sex from me. I found a way to justify all of it, being away from home chasing the big money, sleeping with other women and abusing myself. But in reality I had been a depressed and lonely person.

Only now I realize that what I had really always wanted was to have a simple family life and to be at home every night in bed with my wife. Thankfully, now I can enjoy cooking special dinners for her every night, from braised short ribs to something as simple as baked cod. I make her a cocktail when she gets home from work, and we talk about her day.

Most of all, I am faithful to Beth. My salvation had been at my side for forty years. It just took me a long time to realize it.

EPILOGUE

T his is a memoir of my life with a lot of fiction added to certain storylines to keep you turning the pages. The business events are all mostly factual. I had fun exploring what could have happened with the personal interactions. The characters in the book are all actual people I met along the way. Those that I was still in touch with I contacted and asked them what they wanted their "book name" to be. Many had fun with the idea. A few never responded and I think I know why. Those who didn't respond, or I could not contact, names were changed, of course, to protect the their identities. I am a deeply flawed man who spent years seeking the right path and redemption. I hoped to tell a story, entertain my readers and hopefully relate to others who have had similar struggles in their life. Charles Bukowski finished his novel Post Office saying, "In the morning it was morning and I was still alive. Maybe I'll write a novel, I thought. And then I did." After all my mistakes, here is my book.

ABOUT THE AUTHOR

Ken Owensby grew up in a small town outside of Akron, OH. He holds degrees from the University of Akron and Malone University. He spent a part of his career in computer systems development. He moved to sales/marketing where he had many hard years in corporate sales to financial institutions were not regulated and entertaining was excessive. He went on to be a partner in an Atlanta-based firm and owned his own insurance firm until shortly before retirement. He has been lucky enough to be married to his wife Barb for over forty years and they have one daughter. Due to neurological damage from Chiari Malformation Ken was forced to sell his firm and retire in 2016. He and Barb currently reside in Lancaster, South Carolina.

Made in the USA
Middletown, DE
24 May 2021